Blood in the Bayou

C. M. Sutter

Copyright © 2021
All Rights Reserved

AUTHOR'S NOTE

This book is a work of fiction by C. M. Sutter. Names, characters, places, and incidents are products of the author's imagination or are used solely for entertainment. Any resemblance to actual events or persons, living or dead, is entirely coincidental.

The scanning, uploading, and distribution of this book via the internet or any other means without the permission of the publisher is illegal and punishable by law. Please purchase only authorized electronic editions, and do not participate in or encourage electronic piracy of copyrighted materials. Your support of the author's rights is appreciated.

ABOUT THE AUTHOR

C. M. Sutter is a crime fiction writer who resides in Florida, although she is originally from California.

She is a member of over fifty writing groups and book clubs. In addition to writing, she enjoys spending time with her family and dog, and you'll often find her writing in airports and on planes as she flies from state to state on family visits.

She is an art enthusiast and loves to create gourd birdhouses, pebble art, and handmade soaps. Gardening, bicycling, fishing, and traveling are a few of her favorite pastimes.

C.M. Sutter
http://cmsutter.com/
Contact C. M. Sutter - http://cmsutter.com/contact/

Blood in the Bayou
FBI Agent Jade Monroe - Live or Die Series, Book 1

On her first assignment since her promotion to SSA status in the Serial Crimes Unit of the FBI, Jade Monroe and her new partner, Lorenzo DeLeon, are tasked to southern Louisiana, where disturbing discoveries have been made. Human bones have been found in numerous sites deep in bayou country, and the locals aren't too excited about having outsiders poking around in their business.

When Jade has a chance meeting with a local hunter, she finds his assistance exactly what she needs to break through that unwelcoming barrier. She brings him on board as their go-between.

The hunter inserts himself into their investigation and gains Jade's trust, but is he authentic, or does he have his own agenda?

A bone-chilling blindside and a dangerous chase through the Louisiana swamps is just the beginning, but the question remains—is Jade the hunter, or is she the one being hunted?

See all of C. M. Sutter's books at:
http://cmsutter.com/available-books/

Find C. M. Sutter on Facebook at:
https://www.facebook.com/cmsutterauthor/

Don't want to miss C. M. Sutter's next release?
Sign up for the VIP e-mail list at:
http://cmsutter.com/newsletter/

Chapter 1

Our rented shuttle bus had just arrived at the Crystal Gardens on Navy Pier that Saturday afternoon. It was Jesse and Hanna's big day, and I couldn't have been more excited for them. Although Kate and Amber were better acquainted with Jesse, I'd still known him for more than three years, and I couldn't believe how fast the time had gone.

Our group arriving from North Bend consisted of Kate, Amber, Jack, Billings, Clayton, and myself. At the satellite office in Glendale, we'd picked up Spelling and his wife, Amanda, and J.T.

I looked to the gorgeous summer sky as we parked on Navy Pier and exited the bus. The building's glass atrium glistened in the sunlight.

We were early since Kate was Hanna's maid of honor and rightfully so. She and Jesse had a connection that could never be broken. Kate had been instrumental in saving Jesse's life three years back, and since she couldn't be his best man—Frank had already claimed that position—it was only fitting that Hanna and Jesse asked her to be Hanna's maid of honor. Kate happily accepted.

According to the invitation, everything would be held under one roof, from the exchange of vows and rings to the dinner reception and a night of dancing with a live band. Later, we would spend the night at the Blu Aqua Hotel, a short mile away from the venue. I was sure it would be a wedding to remember.

Kate excused herself to meet up with Hanna and her bridesmaids for pictures before the ceremony. The event was set to begin in an hour.

Our group mingled with other early arrivals, and some I recognized and some I didn't. We joined Jesse's friends at the bar for mimosas. Hugs and handshakes were shared freely between us and Jesse's coworkers. I knew Lutz, Frank, Henry, and Shawn, and I assumed the others were detectives I'd never met. I reintroduced myself to Hanna's mom, Lee, and Jesse's neighbor, Dean, who was Lee's cousin.

At a quarter till four, the announcement came for guests to take their seats. The wedding was set to begin at four o'clock sharp. Everyone was escorted to available seats on both sides of the aisle. There wasn't a groom's side or a bride's side, and the chairs—except for the ones in the first row—were available for anyone to sit wherever they liked. It pulled at my heartstrings to think that Jesse and Hanna had only two family members in attendance—Lee and Dean. I glanced around as I took my seat in the front row with Amber, Jesse's immediate coworkers, his college buddies, and several of Hanna's closest friends from the animal hospital. I was sure that Jesse's heart was full of love as well as sadness. Missing from the front row were his mom, dad, and sister, Jenna, who had been murdered by her own husband three years earlier.

Around us, seats filled quickly. That was how it was in our line of work—cops belonged to a family of brothers and sisters, and the bond of loyalty and support between us ran deep.

That loyalty took me back to our dad's funeral nearly five years ago. The support Amber and I had received from our own community, from surrounding counties, and as far away as California and the San Bernardino County Sheriff's Department, where my dad worked, was beyond belief. I was glad I had brought tissues along and knew I would need them.

Music played as the last guests took their seats. From a room off to the side of the platform appeared Jesse's college buddy Joe, a crime fiction author, and Frank and Dean, and they stood next to the minister. Seconds later, Jesse, dressed elegantly in a black tux, walked up the aisle with Bandit at his side. I dabbed my cheeks with a tissue and handed one to Amber. Jesse and Bandit took their places at the altar, and Jesse gave us a quick smile. Jesse, Frank, and all his buddies rivaled any hot-firefighters calendar lineup, and I considered Hanna a lucky woman.

We watched the end of the aisle and saw Coby enter next. Everyone laughed as he made his way to Bandit's side and sat down obediently. Coby was followed by Kate, who looked radiant in an off-the-shoulder peach-colored mid-calf-length sheath. It beautifully accentuated her tall slender frame. She carried a bouquet of peach-colored tea roses, baby's breath, and lacy ferns. I gave her my biggest grin, and Amber shot a thumbs-up her way as Kate passed. Two other bridesmaids in similar attire followed Kate. The "Wedding March" began, and everyone stood. Phone cameras were at the ready, and seconds later, Hanna walked down the aisle with her mom, Lee. In place of Hanna's father, Lee had the role of giving her daughter away.

Hanna looked stunning. Her long blond hair draped over her shoulders in ringlets, and her headpiece was a tiara with a six-foot-long train that swept the floor. I nearly gasped at the sight of her dress. The sleeveless champagne-colored satin gown had extensive beadwork and the form-fitting style made her look like a goddess. As soon as she appeared from the back of the room, Jesse had tears of what looked like pure love and joy sliding down his cheeks. I could only wish to find love like that again someday. With a sigh, I continued snapping pictures.

After the beautiful ceremony, we gathered again in the bar area while the bride, groom, and wedding party posed for pictures. Amber, Jack, Clayton, Billings, J.T., Spelling, and Amanda took seats at a long banquet table and joined in on conversations with Lutz and Jesse's work crew. We had a lot to catch up on since we hadn't seen each other since football season last year. We exchanged stories for well over an hour. In our line of work, that was something we couldn't help doing.

Lutz tipped his head my way. "Word is you're starting a new job on Monday. Sounds like you got a nice promotion as a senior special agent."

"I did, sir. I'm still in Serial Crimes, but the division I'll be working in has a longer reach. They assist the Manassas, Virginia, unit when needed anywhere in the country, plus they help cover all regions and states east of the Mississippi."

Spelling teased, "Yep, she'll be too good for the likes of us now."

I swatted the air. "Don't even listen to him. The position was offered to J.T. first, but he turned it down."

J.T. laughed. "I like sleeping in my own bed more than three nights a month. Nah, seriously, Jade deserves it."

Lutz chuckled. "Seems like a long drive from North Bend to St. Francis every day."

"It will be, but if I'm in other states and sleeping in hotels half the month, it really won't matter."

"Have you met your new team yet?"

"I did during my orientation, and they all seem great." I jabbed the air. "Much nicer than these dopes."

J.T. pretended to have hurt feelings, and Jack cut in. "You should be used to it, J.T. She dumped us too."

I took my turn. "Well, I can't say that I won't miss all of you because I will." I looked back at Lutz. "Luckily, everyone from my old crew at the sheriff's office lives within ten minutes of me. We see each other a lot, and none of my former FBI buddies live more than forty minutes away. We'll make it work."

Platters of finger food sat at each table, and I munched as we talked. It had been more than eight hours since we'd eaten breakfast back in North Bend.

Amber leaned in at my side. "I just thought of something."

"Yeah, what's that?"

"Kate saved Jesse's life, so they're a lock forever."

"Uh-huh."

"And Frank saved Kate's life. So how does *that* work?"

I raised my brows. "Well, that *is* true."

"Hmm…"

"What does that mean?"

"You know what they say about weddings."

I laughed. "Actually, I don't."

"Just watch as the night plays out. They *are* standing up together, so sooner or later, they'll have to dance together too."

I shook my head. Amber was always the one who played matchmaker. "How old are you now?"

"You know damn well how old I am."

"That's right, so maybe you ought to get out on the dance floor yourself. Who knows? Magic might happen for you too."

She looked around at the crowd and grinned. "There *is* plenty of potential here."

"True, but you live at least a hundred and thirty miles from any of those hunks."

Jack gave me a wink and proceeded to rib Amber. "I'm a single guy and damn good-looking. So what are you saying? I'm nothing more than chopped liver?"

Amber pulled back and wrinkled her nose, then she raised her palms to Jack's face. "Eww, you're my boss and like the brother I never had."

I grinned. "And maybe don't want after all." As we

laughed, I pointed at the group heading our way. "Looks like the wedding party has decided to join us."

Jack rubbed his hands together. "Good. Now maybe the caterers will start setting out the food. I for one am starving."

J.T. nodded. "Make that two of us."

That evening was like the fairy tale we all needed. Our daily lives consisted of seeing and dealing with death, horror, and sadness. Happiness, love, and laughter filled the night and warmed my soul.

After dinner, cake cutting, and the grand march, the band set up, and the music began. Drinks flowed, and people danced. My eyes went to Kate and Frank as they were introduced by the emcee and began a slow dance together. I grinned. Maybe Amber was onto something after all, since they did appear to be enjoying each other's company—a lot.

It was two in the morning by the time the party wound down. The Crystal Gardens was closing up for the night, and most of the guests were either drunk or well on their way. Luckily, plenty of shuttles were waiting outside to take everyone to their hotels.

Jesse and Hanna stood outside the doors as the guests exited. Hugs, kisses, and well-wishes were passed along.

I whispered in Jesse's ear before we boarded the bus. "You did good, dude, and nobody deserves it more than you. I hope you two have a wonderful honeymoon that will last the rest of your lives."

His grin spread to his ears. "That's the plan." He

squeezed my hand and hugged me, Amber, and finally, Kate. "I love you, Kate, and if Hanna and I are lucky enough to have kids someday, and one happens to be a girl, she'll be named Kate, after you."

A lump caught in my throat. I'd never heard such touching words before. Kate and Jesse hugged. She wiped her eyes and kissed his and Hanna's cheeks, then we boarded the shuttle for our hotel. I had a tissue ready for her as we took our seats.

Chapter 2

He couldn't quench his appetite for killing, whether the victim was human or animal. It felt as natural as breathing. Robert Lee Williams—or Robby, as he insisted that the two people he knew call him—had been killing for some time. He justified it as the need to survive—financially and physically. To his surprise, he'd never been caught. To his good fortune, his outdoor skills and his home's location more than guaranteed he would never be discovered. Living deep within the Louisiana bayous, Robby was off the grid, and very few people knew where he lived or even that he existed.

A fall had severely injured his back, resulting in a yearlong forced hiatus and putting his hobby on hold. His food supply was nearly depleted, and his available cash had dwindled to under fifty dollars in the bank. Now that he was back to feeling as strong as he had before, Robby was up to the task, had already completed his fourth kill, and was raring to hit the road that night in search of his next victim.

As he sat on a stump, Robby poked the charred logs, leaned forward, and blew on them. He rubbed his stinging smoke-filled eyes as they began to water, but the embers ignited, and the flames sprang to life. With the stick, he pushed what remained of a hitchhiker's hand back into the flames. Satisfied that it would be nothing but bone fragments and ash soon enough, Robby returned to the stilt shack he shared with three feral cats and a hound dog. He'd had seven cats a year earlier, but he assumed that gators had devoured the others. Robby stirred the stew that had been simmering on the camp stove—he needed to eat something before heading out. Night would fall shortly. He would be on the prowl again, and chances were, he'd invite a new friend home for a late dinner. He also needed to dispose of several carcasses he'd been saving. They needed to be dumped a good distance from his home. It would be easy to toss the human waste into the murky brown water just beyond his door, but he didn't want the gators to become accustomed to the taste of humans. He had no intention of being surprised by an unexpected reptile that could put a quick end to him or Pete, his dog.

He loaded the back of his truck with the carcasses and headed out. Robby anticipated the adrenaline rush that he would experience later that night. He liked to look into his victim's eyes when they realized their fate. With a sniff of the thick Louisiana air, he would catch the scent of fear, and witnessing their last seconds of life exhilarated him. Having that kind of power over another human being gave him strength. He didn't have a vendetta, and he didn't kill for revenge. He killed purely for pleasure, to pocket a few bucks, and to fill his cooler.

Chapter 3

Monday morning had arrived, and my alarm sounded at six o'clock. I needed to be on time for the start of my new position within the FBI. I was excited for the added responsibility, sad to be leaving my old crew, and nervous since I would be the rookie in a group of agents whom I didn't really know. I'd briefly met the person I'd be partnered with, a seasoned agent ten years my senior whose previous partner had taken early retirement and moved to St. Augustine to be closer to family. I couldn't fault anyone who wanted to be near loved ones or to escape the brutal Wisconsin winters that seemed to last for seven months of the year.

A light breakfast of coffee, one over-medium fried egg, and an English muffin was sufficient, and I thanked Amber for making it. She was the cook in the family and a great one at that. The work she and Kate did to keep our home clean and filled with food was appreciated more than they knew.

After eating, I showered, dressed, and grabbed my "go bag." The go bag was as important as our IDs and sidearms, and I needed it ready in case we had to pick up and go at a second's notice. With hugs for confidence, Amber and Kate wished me luck, and I was on my way.

The drive would take just under an hour, and that was without adding traffic in the mix. Research told me that the height of the morning traffic commute and backups was usually between seven thirty and eight o'clock. Hopefully, I would be past the logjam before that happened.

The Milwaukee FBI headquarters was located on the shores of Lake Michigan. The building had recently been erected on Lake Drive in St. Francis, a southern suburb of Milwaukee with a population of just under ten thousand. With Mitchell International Airport only five miles from our bureau, I imagined heading out of state on a case was more than convenient.

I pulled up to the guardhouse at the fence-wrapped facility, stated my name, and showed my badge. I was sure that within a few days, the guard would come to recognize me, and we'd be on a first-name basis. With my credentials verified, I thanked him, continued on after the gate was opened, and followed the signs to the employee parking lot. The building was large and architecturally beautiful—a four-story structure with a tan façade and attractive blue windows. Sitting on the banks of Lake Michigan with sweeping vistas, the building was a monolith in the middle of nowhere.

I hoped to get an office with windows that faced the lake—or at least where I would have such a view from the cafeteria when time permitted. After parking, I crossed the lot, swiped my badge, and stood in front of the retina-based identification screen. After it scanned my eye, the green light flashed, and the door unlocked. Beyond that, there was one more door I had to pass through, but first, I had to enter my own personal four-digit PIN on the keypad. With that done, I put the lanyard holding my ID badge over my neck and took the elevator to the third floor, where I was to meet with my new boss, Supervisory Special Agent Maureen Taft. I'd never reported to a woman before, so it was a new yet exciting experience. From our introductory conversation last week, I'd learned that she was fifty-seven, divorced, and had two children who were on their own. She lived in the Third Ward in a warehouse loft and had worked her way up the ranks over the years, not unlike what I intended to do.

If only Dad were still alive. He'd be so proud.

After reaching the floor I'd be working on, I continued down three hallways and arrived at my boss's office. I sucked in a calming breath, smoothed my pantsuit, and gave the door two raps.

"Come in."

I turned the knob, entered, and waited to be acknowledged.

"Jade, good morning! Excited about your first day?"

"I absolutely am and can't wait to get started."

SSA Taft pushed back her chair and came around the desk. "You've already met Lorenzo, haven't you?"

"I did briefly last week."

"Ah, that's right. Well, first, let's do a quick tour. Everything we use, other than the gym, is on this floor. We have our own lunchroom, locker area, and offices. Let's put away your go bag, refresh your memory as to where the lunchroom is, and then meet up with the team."

"Sounds good." We continued down another hallway of white walls filled with large portraits of FBI directors over the last forty years. An even larger portrait of J. Edgar Hoover, the very first FBI director, hung on the wall at the end of an intersecting hallway. Maureen pushed open a swinging door to a room where things looked more casual. A seating area with a large-screen TV, several table games, and a bookcase filled the left half of the room. The right side opened up into the cafeteria, where at least ten vending machines lined the wall, and several dozen tables with four chairs surrounding each one filled the center of the room.

"Wow, this area is huge."

Maureen nodded. "Yep, and we hold meetings in here, too, at times." She pointed at another door. "In there are the lockers and the restrooms that have showers. There are five restrooms scattered throughout several hallways on this floor, but this is the only one with showers and lockers."

"Got it."

"Okay, let's secure your bag, and then I'll show you to the office you'll be sharing with Lorenzo. Oh, and by the way, you have a nice view of the lake from there."

I wanted to fist pump the air, but instead, I smiled and thanked her. Beyond the cafeteria, we entered the area with the wall placard that read *Ladies*. Inside was a wall of lockers, and beyond that were toilet stalls and showers.

"Grab any available locker. They lock with a personal

four-digit code, so pick out any four numbers. The keys never worked, they always got lost, so we had them swapped out with the keypad system."

"Makes sense." Knowing better than to enter my birth month and year, I entered four random numbers—0591, and that was my locker code. I put my go bag inside and locked the door, and we continued on.

Maureen led the way to the office I'd be sharing with Lorenzo. "The conference room for our team is only two doors down from your office—super convenient."

"That's great." I knew we'd reached the right office when, through the glass wall, I saw Lorenzo sitting at a desk where he looked to be enjoying a cup of coffee and a morning sweet roll. He noticed us, wiped his mouth with a napkin, and waved us in.

"Ready for the big leagues?" he joked.

"I'm more than ready and raring to get started."

He laughed. "There's a lot of research and tedious paperwork that goes along with this killer view."

I let out a deliberate sigh. "Yeah, I bet it's tough."

Maureen turned her wrist and checked the time. "Okay, I'm going to grab a coffee. Conference room at eight thirty sharp."

Lorenzo bit off a piece of sweet roll. "You got it, Boss."

Maureen closed the door at her back. I watched as she walked down the hallway, then I took a seat at my new desk. I felt a twinge of sadness and unfamiliarity. I didn't realize Lorenzo was watching me.

"You'll get used to it."

"What?"

"The new-kid-on-the-block syndrome."

I chuckled. "Is it that obvious?"

"Yep, but it'll go away quickly. We've all experienced it, and it isn't like you're a newbie. You're just a transferee with a more distinguished title."

"Yeah, that's me. What's your title, Lorenzo?"

"Same as yours, kiddo, but with more years under my belt."

I liked Lorenzo. He was ten years my senior, I was told. He had glossy black hair with a little graying at the temples, perfectly straight white teeth, and dimples to die for. He had an average build, but I could tell he worked out. He didn't have that twenty-year-in-the-force belly expansion going on yet. He said he was married to his job, meaning he was single, never had kids, and didn't have a pet—totally free to come and go at a moment's notice, a definite requirement in our line of work.

I opened my desk drawers and saw that they were fully stocked with file folders, pens, a stapler, paper clips, and other supplies. I looked at my new partner. "So what do you go by?"

"As in a name?"

"Yeah."

"Lorenzo DeLeon."

I laughed since it was apparent he didn't use a nickname. "All righty, then. Should we head out?"

"Yep, don't want to keep the boss waiting. She has introductions to make."

Chapter 4

Robby set up a folding camp chair within a few feet of the tree that the barfly was tied to. She was starting to come around. It was early, but Robby always celebrated his hunt with a drink. With a can of cheap beer sitting in the cup holder built into the armrest, the stock of his deer rifle pressed into the dirt, and his hand wrapped around the barrel, he waited to see her expression when she realized she was absolutely and without a doubt royally screwed.

"Open your eyes, baby girl."

Her head flopped and rolled as if it was barely attached. Her long blond hair was matted with twigs, leaves, and dirt. She moaned, most likely from a mix of pain and confusion. Robby was never gentle with his victims. The girl's knees and elbows were bloodied from being dragged through the brush. The tiny skirt she wore to show off her assets was torn, and the heels had broken off her hooker-style boots.

"See what happens when you leave the bar with a stranger? I buy you a half dozen shots and then you're ready to climb into bed with me. Didn't your mama teach you any better than that?" He shook his head as she squinted toward him. "Sluts don't deserve to live, so today, you're going to meet Jesus."

Her eyes opened wide, and his words must have forced her to focus. She jerked left and right and tried to scream, but the ropes securing her arms to the tree and the tape over her mouth prevented her from moving or uttering a sound beyond a moan. Her nostrils flared as she sucked in air.

He nonchalantly pulled her ID card from his pocket. "Let's see here. Your driver's license shows your name is Carla Moline, you're twenty-two, and you live right in Houma." When he noticed she was doing her best to free herself, he snapped his fingers. "Hey! Look at me when I'm talking to you. You aren't going anywhere, so save your energy. Meat is tough when an animal becomes stressed, and I'm a hunter, so I know those things."

Her eyes bulged again, causing Robby to laugh. He stood and walked to the edge of the bank where the swamp took over the solid ground. Only fifteen feet of land separated her from alligator territory. Robby carried the rifle with him in case of a gator ambush.

"There are a lot of alligators in this area, Carla. They have voracious appetites, but me and my critters need to eat too. I'm not a rich man, so I have to live a frugal life. A small gator or a wild pig holds me over for a while, but buying ammo is a luxury I can't often afford, and at times, a man just needs something a little sweeter to eat." He scanned the water and locked on the set of eyes that broke the surface. "Yep, there's a gator ten feet out. Consider yourself lucky, Mr. Gator, since you'll live to see another day."

Robby pulled the flipper knife from his pocket and pressed the tab. The blade shot open. He ran his thumb along the razor-sharp edge as he walked to Carla's side. He stood within inches of her and breathed his hot stench into her face then ripped the tape from her mouth.

"Remember what I said about stress. Now, do you have anything to say?"

Her bloodcurdling scream echoed off the bald cypress trees that grew in the bayou. In a flash, Robby used his right hand to flick the knife across her throat and sever her carotid artery.

"Wrong answer. Now you might as well relax and let nature take its course. You'll be dead in a few minutes."

Robby walked to the cooler then returned to his chair and took a seat. He needed to watch for approaching gators since he was sure they would smell that warm fresh blood. If he had to take a shot to scare one off, he would, but he'd rather save his bullets for emergencies.

It would take a few hours for the water to get to the boiling point in the trough he'd placed over the fire. Meanwhile, he intended to relax, watch Carla fade, and enjoy another beer.

Chapter 5

I had met every person that I'd be directly or indirectly working with. Depending on the need, either two or four agents would assist other divisions. If we were working a case of our own, typically four agents would go out into the field. We had our own computer geek who set up our travel arrangements, forwarded emails and news, and kept us updated on all things relevant to the cases we were currently working on. Maureen's job was to keep the wheels turning at the home base and communicate with the traveling agents each day. Everyone else would assist our St. Francis headquarters or work other cases.

Besides my own partner, Senior Special Agent Lorenzo DeLeon, and our boss, Supervisory Special Agent Maureen Taft, there was Senior Special Agent Tommy Pappas, Senior Special Agent Kyle Moore, Special Agent Charlotte Emery, Special Agent Fay Geddes, Special Agent Mike Flannery, and Special Agent Carl Himes. Every agent had between five and twenty years of experience inside the FBI. We were a group of eight field agents, and I was honored to be with them. I was sure we would become fast friends just as I had with the agents at the Glendale satellite office.

Our computer specialist was Tory Collins, and she'd recently transferred from the Deep South to Milwaukee. I was curious about why since people usually left the northern states to go south for the warmer weather. I'd learned that Tory moved to Wisconsin simply because her fiancé had accepted a new job at Mitchell International as an air traffic controller.

I gave the group a brief look into my personal life and the experiences I'd had in law enforcement—it was a family thing. My father had been a captain at the San Bernardino, California, sheriff's office until his horrific murder five years back. I had been a sergeant at the North Bend Sheriff's Office until I decided to spread my wings and join the FBI. Before his death, my dad used his connections to help me get into the training program immediately. My last three years, I worked as a special agent in Glendale until I was offered the transfer and promotion to the St. Francis position. I told them that my sister, Amber, had started out as a deputy in North Bend but had since been promoted to detective status. Finally, I admitted to being married briefly to my college sweetheart, Lance Keller, and said that I'd remained single since the divorce and we had never had children.

With the introductions complete, Maureen went on to give the daily updates, which consisted of cases still in the works as well as a list of the most dangerous predators nationwide who had been captured during the last twenty-four hours.

After the updates, we filed out of the conference room. Lorenzo bought me a coffee, and we returned to our office, where he promised to share his workload with me.

"How do you get anything done in here with a view like that?" I took my seat and pointed at the sailboat passing by.

"Two ways. The first is by being jacked up by Maureen for not completing assignments when she wants them."

I grinned. "And the other?"

"Like everything else, you get used to the view in time."

I shook my head. "You can get used to this?"

"Yep, but I've had my rear planted in this chair since 2016 when the building opened."

"Ah, I guess that makes sense. So what do you want me to take care of?"

When his desk phone rang, Lorenzo held up his finger, indicating to give him a second. While he spoke on the phone, I set my briefcase on the desk and added a few items from it to my already well-stocked drawers.

"Yep, we're on our way." Lorenzo hung up and stood.

I took that to mean our plans to take care of paperwork had changed.

"Grab your stuff and meet me in Taft's office in five minutes."

I opened my desk drawer and pulled out a pen and notepad.

Lorenzo shook his head. "Not that kind of stuff. Get your go bag. We're heading to Louisiana."

"Oh, shit." I tossed my phone back into my purse, made sure my FBI badge was on my belt and my sidearm in my holster, then I bolted out of the office. Lorenzo was already long gone. I rushed down the hallway to the cafeteria and through the second set of doors. At my locker, I entered 0591 on the keypad then pulled open the door. I slung my go bag over my shoulder, closed the door, and headed to our boss's office. Lorenzo was already inside, his go bag next to him on the floor, and getting briefed by Maureen. I caught my breath as I entered. "I'm ready whenever you are, partner." I looked around. "Just you and me?"

"Yep, just you and me, and I'll explain what we know in the car. Let's go."

"You bet."

Chapter 6

As Lorenzo drove to the FBI's hangar at the airport, I fired off a text to Amber saying that I was on my way to Louisiana, didn't know the details yet, but would fill her in later that night. I silenced my phone so I wouldn't be disturbed as Lorenzo shared what Maureen had learned from law enforcement officials in that area.

"Apparently, human bones have been found around Terrebonne Parish of southern Louisiana this morning. What was passed on to Taft from the Manassas team—who, by the way, won't be joining us—is that they were contacted by the local sheriff's office about bones and pieces of shredded skin found near Houma that looked relatively fresh. It wasn't until *those* bones were found that a red flag was raised."

I frowned. "I'm confused. Why did you emphasize the word *those*?"

"There were others, but the disposal of bodies is sometimes handled differently in that neck of the woods."

"Meaning?"

"Well, in some remote areas, when a person dies, the

family takes things into their own hands and buries the deceased on their property. Of course, over time, the critters find their way to said corpse, dig it up, and gnaw off what remains of the remains."

"That's disgusting."

"It might be to us, but it's somewhat common down in those mostly poor and uninhabited areas."

"So the red flag was because they found more bones today?"

"Sort of."

I sighed. "Okay, what does *that* mean?"

"Law enforcement doesn't think an animal can clean off a body that well in a day or so. There would be much more muscle and skin left behind. Also, animals generally like organ meat if given a choice, but alligators? I guess it depends on how close the remains were to where the gators live. I'd assume an alligator would take full advantage of every piece of the body."

I shook my head. "Then there wouldn't be any remains left."

"That's exactly right, Jade. Another thing that baffles law enforcement is that the bones were found a good five miles from the nearest home."

"No DNA matches of the earlier remains to any missing people in the system?"

Lorenzo shrugged. "I haven't heard all of the details yet, but we'll be briefed once we meet up with the sheriff and his team."

"Okay. So what city are we flying into?"

"New Orleans, and then driving southwest an hour. Tory will text us with the rental car info at the airport, the names of the people we're supposed to meet up with once we get to Houma, and the hotel details there too. I'll forward you what we know so far. That way, you'll have a record of your own."

I nodded then heard my phone buzz. "Guess that's the email coming through."

A half hour later, we lifted off in the FBI's jet. Powering down the runway, taking to the sky, and watching everything beneath us disappear was my favorite part of flying, and having our own jet was definitely better than sitting in a coach seat on a commercial airliner while being elbowed by strangers. In two and a half hours, we would be on the ground again, and while in the air, I'd have a snack and coffee and look over the report. There was a chance I'd even catch an hour of shut-eye. Since I didn't know Lorenzo well, I had no idea what his habits or personality traits were like, but I was sure to learn more about him during this first trip and case we were working together.

Reading what Lorenzo had sent me took about as long as the explanation he'd given me as he drove to the airport. The only additional things stated in the report were the names of the sheriff and several deputies. I was sure the name tags on their shirts would help us if there was any confusion.

When I looked up from my phone, I smiled. Lorenzo had already dozed off. I wasn't surprised since every male partner I've had over the years could zonk out in minutes. I put away my phone and stared out the window. A patchwork of colorful farmland lay beneath us, and I felt like I could reach out and touch the beautiful cloud formations that floated by. I would never get tired of being among the clouds and enjoying the earth's beauty from a perspective above it. I closed my eyes and drifted off.

"Jade?"

I tried to open my eyes, but they weren't cooperating. I tried again and squinted at the face only inches from me. When my focus cleared, I saw it was Lorenzo, and I quickly sat up. "I hope to God I wasn't drooling."

He laughed. "The front of your blouse is soaked."

I looked down in horror and realized he was joking. I grinned and knew we would get along just fine. "You got me on that one."

He sat down and fastened his seat belt. "You were snoring, though."

I swatted the air. "There's a chance I'd believe that since I've been told that before." I glanced out the window, and we were descending. "Are we here already?"

"Yep. The pilot said we'd be on the ground in fifteen minutes. Thought you might want to freshen up a little before we deplane."

"I do, and thanks." I unfastened my belt, pushed off the arm of the seat, and walked to the lavatory. Inside, I splashed water on my face, tore open a prepackaged toothbrush and a miniature tube of toothpaste, and brushed my teeth. I fluffed my hair and considered my appearance good enough. I would give myself a thorough once-over in our hangar's ladies' room. Back in my seat, I looked out the window at the runway in the distance. We would be touching down in seconds. As I snapped my seat belt, I heard the wheels being lowered. With a slight jostle, the jet was on the runway and screeched to a stop. We taxied to the private hangars and stopped on the tarmac where we'd wait for the door to open and stairs to be lowered. Lorenzo and I stood, grabbed our go bags, and waited at the door.

The copilot turned the door latch and lowered the stairs. "You're good to go, Agents."

With a nod, I thanked him, and we deplaned. Several vehicles were parked to the left of the hangar, and I assumed one was our rental. We would go inside, confirm it, and use the restrooms before leaving.

"I got an update from Tory while you were sleeping."

"Yeah, what's that?"

He chuckled. "We aren't in New Orleans."

I frowned. "Then where the hell are we?"

"Turns out that Houma does have its own regional airport. We were cleared to continue on and fly right into Houma. I guess the city of Houma is about six miles away."

"Awesome. That's a heck of a lot closer than doing the hour drive from New Orleans."

After confirming that the Explorer outside was our rental, we grabbed coffees to go, used the facilities, and left.

"So should we check in at the hotel first and then go to the sheriff's office?"

"Sounds like a good idea. We don't know how far it is from town to the remains, so I guess a deputy will lead us there once we check in with them. The sheriff, several deputies, and a forensic unit are at the site right now and will stay there until we arrive. They want to preserve as much of the scene as they can, but their location sounds like the kind of place that wouldn't come up on Navigation. Too far out in the boondocks."

"Hence the escort. So how were the remains discovered?"

Lorenzo scratched his cheek. "That information hasn't come down the pike yet, at least not to us."

I pondered something as we loaded our gear into the Explorer. "Would you mind if I called you something else?"

Lorenzo's eyebrows shot up. "You mean besides my name?"

I laughed. "Yeah. Why be so formal? We are partners, you know."

"Hmm… so what do you have in mind?"

I shrugged. "Something shorter, maybe? How about Renz?"

He pulled back. "You'd be removing the front and back end of my name?"

"Yeah, I guess." I smiled. "I like it. Sounds kind of edgy—Renz DeLeon."

He cocked his head. "I kind of like it too. Okay, sure. You can call me Renz."

I was happy. We were making progress.

"Just one question."

"Sure, go for it."

"What can I call you?"

"Jade."

We both laughed, and Renz followed the sign for downtown Houma.

Chapter 7

Robby had to take a trip into Houma that afternoon. It was Monday, and his meager monthly hunting land lease payment from the state—one hundred eighty dollars—would have been direct deposited into the bank by then. He needed to pull out some money. Having the pickup full of gas guaranteed that when he got the itch, he could go hunting and pocket even more cash. It made no difference to him whether he killed men or women, even though he preferred women since they were easier to subdue. It was how they filled his needs that mattered.

He counted his remaining bullets to make sure he had enough to last until he got paid next month. He was good.

After the broken screen door slammed at his back, Robby walked to the firepit and checked the water temperature in the trough. It had begun a slow simmer and would soon be boiling. He jammed another log in the fire then headed for the tree to cut down Carla.

"Son of a bitch!" Robby yelled and threw a rock at the gator that had already devoured Carla from the hips down. The gator spun and hissed. Robby ran to the house and grabbed his rifle from against the cooler where he'd last left it. He took aim and fired off two rounds as he closed in on the enormous reptile. Mud shot up—he'd missed. The gator slunk into the murky water and disappeared. "Damn you!" Robby inspected what was left of the woman and decided not to take the chance of keeping any of her carcass since the alligator's claw marks covered her body. "That's a crying shame, and now I have to throw away what's left of her. I'm not taking any chances with tainted meat. You never know what kind of germs and bacteria are under the claws of those hideous critters."

After taking a careful look around to make sure no other opportunists were headed his way, Robby cut down what remained of the woman, dragged her by the wrists to the trough, and submerged her in the boiling water. Pete, the hound, was already drooling.

Once he'd arrived home late last night, Robby had emptied Carla's purse and tossed it and her phone into the firepit. As he stood at the fire and pocketed her cash, all that remained in her wallet was her license and credit cards. Robby wouldn't let himself be tempted by those cards—he wasn't about to invite trouble with a paper trail. He tossed the wallet into the fire and headed to the truck. The plan was to make a quick stop on his way to town and peek at the remains he'd gotten rid of. He'd been excited to get to town last night and find somebody to take home with him. That excitement might have caused him to commit a careless act in dumping that much waste in one location. If all of it was ever found, it would be obvious—unless the animals had carried everything away—that there would likely be several skulls, rib cages, and other duplicate bones in the same area. He hoped that the animals that called the bayou home had eaten every morsel of evidence that he'd left behind last night.

The drive to Houma would take a little longer because of the detour west to reach the dump site. Robby intended to be in and out in less than fifteen minutes. What was once a gravel driveway had become overgrown, reduced to a path and nearly hidden in the tree cover. It would take him a half mile in before it dead-ended. The bayou took over at that point, and a walk through the thicket would take another five minutes before he reached the site.

After a number of S-shaped turns on Falgout Canal Road, Robby made a sharp right onto Bayou Dularge Road. The path he would turn onto was ten minutes farther north and on the right. Sprinkled along the route were a handful of dwellings, but most had seen better days, and the ones still standing looked uninhabitable. Some had been abandoned years earlier, and what remained were only broken frames and shells of what used to be homes. Robby passed them without a second look—he'd seen them all before. He slowed about a half mile out. The path was easy to miss, and the landscape everywhere looked the same.

Except for that. What the hell is going on?

His back stiffened, and he leaned in closer to the windshield as he approached the flashing lights. Robby was sure his eyes were playing tricks on him.

That can't be—not a cop car!

He balled his hand and pounded the steering wheel as he cursed his luck.

Keep your cool, asshole. You don't want to draw attention to yourself.

As Robby checked his speed, he tapped the brakes. He didn't intend to give the cops a single reason to pull him over. He continued on and passed the deputy's vehicle then turned at the next right. That path continued even deeper into the marshlands, and he drove until the truck was dangerously close to soggy ground and brush. Getting stuck back there wasn't an option. Robby killed the engine and climbed out, then he grabbed the binos from behind the seat. He quietly closed the driver's-side door and took to the woods on foot. He needed to get close enough to see what was going on but not so close that he would be noticed. The binoculars would help him stay hidden while trying to find out if the carcasses had been discovered. Tracking south through the brush nearly a quarter mile would get him close enough to see and hear most everything. A lifelong resident of the bayous, Robby was a skilled hunter and tracker and knew how to maneuver the swamps unseen.

Making sure to stay on the animal paths that zigzagged through the dry areas and wetlands, he closed in on the scene that had unfolded at the end of the path he'd thought was a sure bet. How those remains had been discovered was puzzling and something he needed to know. With that new information, he would have to tweak his methods of disposal going forward.

Maybe I should rethink this process. I might have to toss

every bit of waste in the bayou behind the shack, anyway. No evidence would ever lead back to me, but I'd still have to deal with those damn gators.

Robby lifted the binos to his eyes and adjusted the focus until the scene before him was crystal clear. Two cars from the sheriff's office were parked single file on the path, and behind them sat a black van with the words Terrebonne Parish Forensic Department written across the side in white lettering.

Damn it. They must have found the bones, but who's that parked farther in?

Robby scanned slightly left, and twenty feet ahead of the first deputy's car was a red pickup truck with several empty cages in the bed. Sitting on the tailgate were two men, and by all appearances, they looked to be local. One was talking on his phone. Robby studied the cages, which were large enough for a half dozen hunting dogs—Catahoulas, he presumed. There wasn't any other explanation for being back there in the middle of nowhere. They were hunters who'd brought their dogs out in search of wild boars and happened upon the remains.

Somebody must have picked up the dogs. Otherwise, they'd be barking up a storm.

Robby thought about his chances of being discovered—they were slim to none. He wasn't in the system and was something of a recluse. People didn't stop by and visit, and few even knew of his stilt shack back there among the wetlands unless they came by on a boat. Robby's guests were on a short list, and their lives were even shorter.

He headed to his truck. There was nothing he could do to change the outcome. He planned to go into town, hit the bank, then drive home the same way to see if the sheriff and his team were still there.

Chapter 8

We passed the city-of-Houma population sign at twelve thirty. With nearly thirty-three thousand residents, the town was larger than I'd expected.

Renz glanced across the seat at me. "Do you have anything in your go bag that isn't business attire? We'll likely be on swampy ground."

I grinned as a memory popped into mind. "I learned my lesson years ago. If there's a disgusting place to trudge through, I've done it, *and* while wearing heels. Believe me, I've got everything jammed into that go bag, including rubber boots."

"How about bug spray?"

I snapped my fingers. "Damn, that's one thing I didn't bring."

"You've got a long-sleeved shirt?"

"I sure do."

"Okay, let's check in and then change into more appropriate clothes for trudging through disgusting places." He passed his phone to me. "Read Tory's last text and see what hotel she booked for us."

"No problem." I tapped the message icon and read the last text that Tory had sent. "Let's see. She said we have two singles reserved at the HomeStay Inn. The address is 102 Library Drive."

"Good enough. Want to program that into the infotainment center?"

"Sure." I entered the hotel name on the screen, and a red teardrop came up showing the hotel's location. "There, we're good to go."

After weaving through town, we arrived at the hotel, grabbed our bags, and checked in. The elevator took us to the second floor, where we had rooms 203 and 205. We agreed to meet in the lobby in fifteen minutes. My room was typical of the less-than-one-hundred-dollars-a-night variety. It was clean, well appointed, and roomy enough with a table, two chairs, a queen-sized bed, and a credenza that acted as a coffee and microwave bar, TV stand, and dresser. A closet with plenty of hangers and a nice-sized bathroom were near the exit door.

This will be just fine, but for now, I need to change clothes and get downstairs. I'll hang up everything later when we get back.

I dumped the contents of my go bag onto the bed and separated the tops from the bottoms and the shoes from the rubber boots. I slipped into a pair of khakis and a long-sleeved white T-shirt, put on a pair of flats, and pulled my hair back into a ponytail. After jamming a pair of socks into the boots, I fired off a quick text to Amber saying only that we had arrived and I would update her later, then I grabbed my purse and room key and left. I didn't see Renz in the hallway, so I assumed he was already waiting in the lobby.

Downstairs, I walked up on a conversation between the reservations agent and Renz. He was asking for directions to the sheriff's office, and once he had them, he thanked the agent, and we left.

"Got it figured out?" I asked as I fastened my seat belt.

"Yep, it looks like we have to backtrack to Main Street. Probably eight blocks or so."

I handed Renz a candy bar. "Like Snickers?"

"I love Snickers." He tore open the wrapper and took a bite, and I did the same. "Where'd you get them?"

"From the vending machine at the end of the hallway. It's right next to the ice machine on our floor. Oh, and just an FYI for future reference."

He raised his brows. "Yeah, what?"

"Snickers is my favorite candy bar, now and forever."

He laughed. "Good to know."

We reached the sheriff's office a few minutes later. According to the text from Tory, we were supposed to ask for a deputy named Steven Polsen. Renz parked in an open spot in their lot, and we headed to the main entrance. The stark-white concrete building stood out like a sore thumb. It was butted up to the street like an afterthought and was jammed next to houses, churches, and apartment buildings.

"Not the loveliest place," I joked as Renz pulled open the glass door and allowed me through.

The two female deputies who sat behind a counter only thirty feet away looked up as we entered. We approached them, pulled out our IDs, and said we were there to meet with Deputy Polsen.

"Sure thing, Agents, and I know he's expecting you. I'll go get him."

Renz sat in a grouping of several couches and waited. I poured two coffees from their coffee bar, took a seat across from Renz, and handed one to him.

"Is black okay? I didn't see any creamer there."

"Black is fine. Thanks."

Five minutes later, the door behind the counter opened, and a man who appeared to be around thirty walked out. He was dressed in a deputy's typical tan uniform and crossed the lobby with his hand outstretched.

"Agents DeLeon and Monroe, I presume? I'm Deputy Polsen. Nice to meet you."

Renz introduced both of us, then we walked out with Polsen.

"Do you want to follow me or ride together?"

"How far away is the site?" I asked.

He scratched his forehead. "I'd say it's about ten miles south of town."

Renz spoke up. "We'll go ahead and follow you, then." He pointed at our rental. "That black Explorer is our vehicle."

"Sure thing. Just go ahead and pull up behind me."

We were on our way a few minutes later with Polsen in the lead.

"Sticky as hell this time of year." Renz ran his handkerchief across his forehead.

"Then it's lucky for you that I'm your partner."

The left side of his mouth curled up and formed a cockeyed grin. "Really, and why's that?"

I pulled a pack of travel wipes from my purse and handed one to him. "Because I may have forgotten the bug spray, but at least I brought these, and they're refreshing."

He thanked me and dabbed his face with the wipe as I adjusted the A/C vents to point toward him.

"Ah, that feels great. Thanks, Jade."

I nodded and watched as the landscape passed my window. The city we'd left disappeared quickly as I checked my side mirror. The road narrowed, and flora had taken over everything right up to the paved road.

"Wow, it turns rural really fast." Behind the houses next to the road, I looked for signs of a clearing in the tree cover, but it was nearly impossible. I couldn't even imagine walking through that thick tangle of who knew what. "It's really dense back there."

Renz glanced out his window and nodded. "Yep, it sure is. I bet there are all kinds of critters in those woods that no sane person would want to deal with. The ground is likely soggy, there are probably snakes hanging from trees, wild boars roaming around, and then close to the water would be the enormous gators." He grinned when I shuddered. "Lions and tigers and bears, oh my! What? Not a fan of nature, Agent Monroe?"

"I am as long as I'm on a paved bike or running trail."

The drive took under twenty minutes since it was a straight shot out of town to reach the site. Deputy Polsen's brake lights flashed, then he slowed down at the Terrebonne Parish deputy's car parked at the entryway to the gravel path. We waited behind the deputy as the two men had a brief conversation through open car windows.

"I wonder what's going on?"

Renz shrugged.

A second later, Polsen climbed out of his car and walked to our vehicle.

"I guess we're about to find out." Renz lowered his window and stuck out his head. "What's up?"

"There isn't room back there for this many vehicles. Go ahead and park on the shoulder. I'll do the same, and Stillman said he'd drive us back there."

"Sounds good."

Renz pulled ahead and parked on the shoulder while I slipped on my rubber boots and pocketed my cell phone and wipes. We climbed out at the same time, then he clicked the fob and locked the Explorer's doors. Polsen parked at our rear bumper, and together, we climbed into Stillman's squad car. He drove down the overgrown path to its end, where the area was already crowded with vehicles. Polsen, Renz, and I exited the deputy's car and thanked him, then he backed down the path.

Polsen tipped his head toward the people standing alongside the forensic van. "Come on. I'll introduce you to the sheriff and our forensic team." Renz and I followed.

"SSA Lorenzo DeLeon and SSA Jade Monroe, this is the Terrebonne Parish sheriff, Pat Conway."

We walked up to a man who looked to be in his fifties

with buzz-cut gray hair and a protruding belly. We reached out and received a hearty handshake.

Even though I had been with the FBI for a number of years, I was new to our team and thought it more respectful for Renz to lead the questioning. I was curious to see how he led an investigation, anyway.

Renz began by asking about the men who sat on the truck's tailgate.

"They're the guys who discovered the remains. They were out here boar hunting with their Catahoulas, and the dogs sniffed out those bones immediately. The man on the right, who owns the dogs, is Billy Bennett, and he said they'd only been out here for a few minutes before they called it in."

Renz looked around. "So what happened to the dogs?"

"They were transferred to another truck and taken out. They were trampling the scene, and we didn't want them to"—the sheriff wrinkled his face—"eat the evidence."

I cringed at the thought. "Smart thinking."

"Anyway, the dogs were making such a ruckus, we couldn't think straight. The guys stayed behind since I was sure you'd probably want to question them."

Renz glanced their way. "And we'll get to that shortly. So we were called in because other sites similar to this one have been found scattered throughout the parish?"

"That's correct, but we originally thought they were from 'at-home' burials. This one"—he shook his head—"is only a day or two old, and there's more than one set of bones."

I looked around. "Not to mention there wouldn't be a reason to bury remains way back here off the beaten path."

"That's right, Agent Monroe, but the fact is they weren't buried, not even partially. It's as if this is a dump site."

Renz pointed toward the footpath. "Is the scene back there?"

Sheriff Conway tipped his head in that direction. "It is."

"Then let's go take a look."

Chapter 9

My head was on a swivel as we plowed along spongy ground through the brush and vines covering the narrow trail.

"Do gators come in this far?" I asked, thankful that we were all armed.

Polsen spoke up. "They don't have a reason to, and with their low, heavy bodies, it would be tough to maneuver this thicket."

I breathed a sigh of relief. "Then what uses this path?"

"Wild hogs, mostly, and of course, the men and dogs that hunt them. Don't get too comfortable, though. There are plenty of snakes out here too."

My rubber boots squeaked with every step, and my eyes darted left and right. "How much farther?"

"Another minute or two. We're close."

When I saw yellow tape wrapped around tree trunks to outline the area, it was obvious that we'd arrived at the spot. I immediately understood what the sheriff had meant when he said the dogs could have quickly destroyed the scene. The spot stank, hundreds of flies and bugs covered the rotting tissue that hung from the bones, and in the heat and humidity, the scent would easily attract opportunistic animals.

Conway pointed. "Luckily, we're a good distance from the water. Otherwise, the gators would have literally eaten every bit of evidence." He pointed to his far right. "And those would have been gone forever."

I wrinkled my nose at the two skulls lying in the damp soil, walked around the tape, and knelt to get a closer look. I pulled out my cell phone and snapped a few pictures.

"Forensics took plenty of photographs already that will be available to you."

I looked over my shoulder. "Thanks, but I like to have some of my own for quick reference." I glanced at one of the forensic techs, who was easily identified by the logo on his shirt. "Can you tell by the skulls if these body parts belong to women or men?"

"Not so much by the skulls, but the length of the femurs would tell us how tall the victim was so likely their gender too."

"How about dental records?"

"We can certainly work with those if anything unusual stands out."

Renz looked at me. "As well as the missing persons database." He addressed the sheriff next. "Has anyone been reported missing, say, in the last few weeks?"

"Several people have, and one was found just last week in New Orleans. Local police had picked up a sixteen-year-old who was soliciting herself on a street corner. Turns out, she was one of the missing people and had run away. She's back home and under the close watch of her mama. She's one of the lucky ones, even though she may not think of it that way."

I pushed off my knee and stood. "Lucky in what way?"

The sheriff blew out a hard breath. "Many of the teen runaways get snatched up in the illegal world of human trafficking. The runaways are approached by men who spin an attractive lie and tell them everything they want to hear—big-city life, great jobs, and a support network—just to be handed off to a trafficker for money or drugs, and the girls are never seen again. Unfortunately, because many areas of the South are poor, those girls want to leave the bayou and go to the big city. They believe everything they're told." He gestured with his hands. "Poof. Then they're gone and never seen again."

Renz frowned. "So if that's the case, then why would those bones be from runaways? Dead girls don't bring in money."

Conway shrugged. "Not saying they are, but there could be a connection."

I took my turn. "How far away were the locations of the other bones? Were they found in the same parish, and what happened to them?"

"They were, Agent Monroe. Terrebonne Parish is one of the largest parishes in Louisiana and covers a lot of land. Our medical examiner has the remains on cold storage so they won't deteriorate any further."

Renz spoke up. "We'll have to take a look at those, too, when we get back to Houma."

I circled the site and snapped off a dozen more pictures of a heap of bones that still had tissue on them. It was a macabre sight. I nodded to Renz that I'd seen enough. I addressed the forensic team before heading toward the vehicles. "One more thing. Can you tell which bones go with which?"

Toby Cordon from Forensics answered. "We can, ma'am, by running the DNA."

"Okay, good, and thank you. How soon will these bones be in your lab?"

"We'll be removing them right away. We've already collected what we need from the scene, so check back with us in a few hours. We should have everything in the lab by then."

We returned to where the vehicles were parked and approached the men who still sat on the truck's tailgate.

Renz took the lead. "Sorry to detain you fellas for so long. I'm sure you've been out here for a few hours."

"Yep. Not what we expected to be doing today."

"I bet. Let's get started, then, so you guys can be on your way. I'll take your names and addresses, and then together, you can walk us through the chain of events."

They agreed and gave us their names as Mark LaFleur and Billy Bennett before sharing their addresses. I would take on the responsibility of writing down their account of the day. With my notepad and pen in hand, I nodded a go-ahead.

Mark began with the time they'd arrived—eight fifteen that morning. Their intention was to spend a good portion of the day hunting like they usually did when they went out. They began their normal routine, which was to release the dogs to hunt and follow them with their GPS trackers. If a feral pig was located, the dogs would surround it, bark up a storm, and wait until the owner arrived to shoot it—a relatively foolproof act.

"So you had released the dogs, and within minutes, they started howling?"

"They did," Billy said, "but they weren't chasing anything, which was unusual. The GPS showed that their movement had stopped, so it didn't take us long to catch up with them."

I was afraid to ask the next question, but I had to. "Did you see them eat anything?"

Billy continued. "I didn't actually see that, but they were sure sniffing and digging. Once we realized what they were excited about, we pulled out the dogs, caged them, and called 911. Guess those remains could be compromised somewhat by the dogs."

"How many dogs did you have?" Renz asked.

"We brought out five this morning," Billy said. "My wife came and picked them up since they were too excited and loud."

"Understood, and we sure do appreciate your quick thinking to preserve that evidence."

Mark rubbed the sweat from his forehead. "I've never seen anything like that before, and I'm actually surprised the pigs didn't smell it."

My curiosity was piqued. "Why would that matter?"

"Wild pigs can devour human body parts in a matter of minutes."

I pulled back. "But I thought that was—"

Mark chuckled. "An urban legend?"

"Well, yeah."

"No, ma'am. They're dangerous animals, especially when injured, and fast as hell. If we shoot at them, we'd better take good aim and shoot them dead. They'd be hot on our trail and make short work of us otherwise. They have razor-sharp teeth and tusks."

"And here I thought pigs ate hay and grain. Damn. No, thanks."

Billy chuckled before adding a final comment. "There's two things I know for sure, though."

Renz raised a curious brow. "Yeah, what's that?"

"The first is those remains couldn't have been out there more than a day. The pigs would have found them and devoured them by now. I'm sure the only reason they didn't is because our dogs and all the commotion this morning caused them to keep their distance."

"And the other thing?"

Billy scratched his cheek. "The person you're looking for is definitely a hunter. He can cut up and remove the meat from the bones of a human as well as from a pig."

I groaned under my breath. "For what purpose?"

Billy shook his head. "God only knows."

I sucked in a deep breath and blew it out then turned to Renz. "Have enough info for now?"

"Yep." He handed cards to both guys. "We sure

appreciate you hanging out here and waiting for us to arrive. If anything else comes to mind, please don't hesitate to call. We'll probably be in town all week."

They pocketed the cards and jumped off the tailgate.

I looked at the line of vehicles blocking the path. "How are you going to get out of here?"

Billy smiled and opened the driver's-side door. "In four-wheel drive."

I turned to Sheriff Conway after the guys left. "Is there a room at the sheriff's office that we can work from?"

"You bet. Hop on in. I'll give you a ride back to your vehicle."

Minutes later, we left with the sheriff and his deputies. The forensic team stayed behind to collect all the bones and bag them then do a final sweep of the area for anything that could be of evidentiary value. They would return to their lab and start identifying which bones went together by using DNA testing. Luckily for us, the lab was only three miles from the sheriff's office.

Once we arrived, Sheriff Conway directed us to a small interview room to use as our office during our stay in Houma. We would compile the information gathered by the sheriff's office, the forensic lab, and ourselves and forward it to our FBI specialists.

After asking for a good restaurant recommendation, Renz and I temporarily parted ways with the sheriff. It was pushing five o'clock, and we were starving. He suggested Nina's if we wanted authentic creole cuisine, and it happened to be only two blocks from the sheriff's office and a straight shot down Lafayette Street to our hotel. We thanked him and left. We planned to have an early supper then pay the forensic lab a visit after that. We also needed to take a look at the bones that were found in the last few weeks and see how they compared to the ones discovered earlier that day, but first, dinner was on the menu.

Chapter 10

Robby was fuming. His dump site had been discovered, but because the location was so remote and off the beaten path, he knew the people who'd found it had to be hunters.

I'll show them a thing or two about hunting. The last thing I need is people up in my business when I'm just trying to get by. They'll pay in the end. They want wild boars, I'll find a way to give them wild boars.

Robby stared at the trough. The meat was thoroughly cooked, but because that gator had torn it up, it would now be considered dog and cat food. He wasn't about to eat anything that could be filled with swamp and gator bacteria.

As he sat in the shack and pondered what he'd come across earlier, he knew he would have to change the way he disposed of the waste. He could no longer take the chance of scattering bones throughout the parish. Law enforcement was involved, and there was a good chance they would start patrolling the paths that led to the swamps. Going forward, he planned to feed the remains to either the gators or the boars. He was sure his chances against a wild pig were far better than with a gator, and if he dumped the remains on his own property but far enough away from his living quarters, he'd be safe. He looked into the simmering water and cursed. That meat would have tasted mighty fine, but at least he had the fifty dollars from her wallet and another seventy-five he'd withdrawn from the bank.

His stomach growled, and a thought popped into his head. Monday was ladies' night at Nina's, and the drinks were two for one. Robby tipped his wrist and checked the time—5:03.

Happy hour is between four and six. Maybe I should head out and see what's on the menu.

The drive to Nina's from the outskirts of Dulac, where he lived, would take a half hour. He needed to hurry. After happy hour, his choices of women to become acquainted with and follow throughout the night would diminish quickly.

Instead of pulling the cooked meat out of the trough and cutting it up for the animals, Robby left it where it was, washed up, and hit the road in his truck. He'd cleaned his flipper knife, which was deep in his pocket and ready to be used again.

Robby arrived at the restaurant shortly after five thirty. He entered and took a seat at the counter, where two women sat with several cocktails lined up in front of them. One or both of the women would be good candidates for later. He ordered a beer and took in the room. The door opened just as he was about to strike up a conversation with the ladies. The tan uniform gave the man away—it was the deputy who'd stood outside his car when Robby drove past the path earlier.

That son of a bitch is about to ruin my plans. I can feel it already.

Robby kept his head down and his ears perked. He saw the deputy approach a couple who were seated in a booth directly to Robby's right. He nonchalantly glanced that way and listened as the conversation began.

"Agents DeLeon and Monroe. Looks like somebody gave you a good recommendation for supper."

The female spoke up. "Deputy Stillman. This must be a popular restaurant, and according to the sheriff, it's one of the best in town."

"He's absolutely right. Have you ordered yet? The po' boys are great."

"We have," the male agent said. "We're getting a combo platter of shellfish and seafood."

"Well, you can't go wrong with that either. I passed the lab on my way here. Looks like the forensic van is back."

"Good to know," the female said, "and that's our next stop before we call it a day."

The deputy tipped his head. "Have a nice night, and I'll probably see you tomorrow." He took a seat on the other side of the women at the counter.

Robby gave the agents a long hard look before gulping down his beer and starting the second one.

Agents, huh? That has to mean the FBI, and they'd only be involved if the other dump sites were discovered. I need to find out what they know and then stay one step ahead of them. Guess I'll be rummaging through those other spots tomorrow. If all the bones are gone, then it's possible they've been scooped up by law enforcement. But with any luck, those agents will leave town, and the bones found in Louisiana will just be another case they couldn't solve.

Disappointed that his plans for the night wouldn't go forward, Robby had nothing but time on his hands. He guzzled a second beer, settled his tab, left a handful of change on the counter as a tip, and walked out. He climbed into his truck and watched. As luck would have it, he had a bird's-eye view through the glass walls of the restaurant. He saw the agents sitting at their booth. They'd be done eating sooner or later, then Robby would follow them until they ended their night.

Chapter 11

We'd finished our delicious sampling of authentic creole cuisine and left the restaurant. The forensic lab and medical examiner's office would be our final stop for the night. Tomorrow, we planned to forward what we had to our team then spend the day talking to people out and about in the areas where the bones were found to see if they had any information for us. Someone had to be familiar with a local individual known to be weird, reclusive, aggressive, and most likely mentally challenged. We would make the rounds, talk to hunters, and go from there. The killer was either seriously disturbed or an extremely dangerous man with a fetish for murdering and reducing a human to nothing but bones and chunks of tissue. The image was sickening, but with feet on the ground and by asking plenty of questions, we could get lucky.

With Renz behind the wheel, we headed to the forensic lab a few miles away and met up with Toby Cordon and Hal Petrie, the forensic techs. We thanked them for staying late to accommodate us.

"So, we realize it's too soon to have a definitive answer on which bones go together, but can you tell us if they're from two bodies, three bodies, or what?"

Toby nodded. "Yes, just because we found two skulls doesn't mean there were only two bodies, but we have counted the bones and matched them the best we could by color, density, and size. We're pretty confident that there were only two bodies at that particular dump site."

"And the previous dump sites?" I asked.

"The first discovery was reported, and deputies checked it out, but it was assumed that the bones might have originally been from a home burial and were scattered by wild animals. They were discolored by the peat soil and badly chewed on. The only house in the area had been abandoned long before, so we had nobody to ask."

I frowned. "What about the skull?"

"None was ever found there, ma'am."

Renz took his turn. "And the second site?"

"Similar to the one we found today. Located by hunters and called in. That was also a one-body find—no skull there either, but it raised a red flag. We were able to determine that those bones were fresh—less than a week old. We didn't find an entire skeleton of bones, just some here and there in a general twenty-foot-square area. We'd assumed the critters beat us to them."

"Were there cut marks that separated the bones?"

"No, ma'am. The bones were separated at the ligaments. Some tendons remained, but most of the muscle had been cut away."

"Hmm… are there butcher shops in the area?" Renz asked.

"There are, Agent DeLeon, but I'd concur with what those hunters said earlier today. The person you're looking for is a hunter, yet he's as skilled as any trained butcher. There are a few slight scrapes and nicks on the bones, likely from the knife used to remove the muscle."

"And you can compare those markings to the bones you've collected from the other sites?" I asked.

"Yes, ma'am, but we won't get to that until tomorrow."

Renz seemed satisfied. "Okay, we'll leave you to it, then. There's no reason for us to hang around, but if you do find comparable marks on the bones, we'd like to see them."

"You bet, and I'll give you a call as soon as we know something."

I added that we would be out and about tomorrow questioning people in the area, but if they saw similarities, we could head back immediately. "Oh, we don't even have the locations of where the other bones were found."

Hal spoke up. "Give me a second, Agent Monroe, and I'll print that out for you."

With the sheet of paper in hand and a thank-you, we headed to the door.

"Agents?"

We both turned.

"Yep?" Renz said.

"Be careful out there. Some of those bayou people are very reclusive and don't like intruders."

I frowned. "But—"

"It's just a friendly warning. There are strange folks back there."

I shivered as we walked to our vehicle.

Renz noticed. "There's no way in hell you're cold, are you?"

"No, just creeped out a little."

Renz laughed. "What's that on your hip?"

I looked down and chuckled too. "My Glock."

"And you are?"

I played along as I pulled open the passenger door of the Explorer. "Jade Monroe, a senior special agent in the FBI's Serial Crimes Unit."

"And a kickass tough woman from everything I've heard, so don't forget it."

"Yes, sir, SSA Lorenzo DeLeon."

Chapter 12

Robby finally smashed the mosquito that had been pestering him for the last few minutes. His own blood and a dead bug covered a dime-sized area on the back of his hand. He smeared it on his pant leg before rolling up the truck window. He'd heard enough, and it was exactly what he'd suspected ever since he'd seen those strangers talking to the deputy in the restaurant.

"So, you're a special agent with the FBI, are you? Well, la-di-da. I'll definitely show you what special treatment feels like if you get in my way. I guaran-damn-tee it."

He remained low in his seat until the agents reached the stop sign a block ahead. Robby turned the key in the ignition and followed them through town. When the male agent clicked the blinker and turned onto Library Drive, Robby knew exactly where they were going—the HomeStay Inn. He slowed to a crawl and didn't turn in until they had parked alongside the building and exited the vehicle. When they reached the door, he drove past them.

"Looks like your rooms are somewhere on this side of the building." After making sure there weren't any cameras facing the side lot, he backed into the spot next to theirs. Soon enough, he would see lights go on in one or two of those rooms. He craned his neck as he stared up at the wall of windows.

"There!" He counted the windows from the end of the building to the room that had just lit up on the second floor—six windows.

Six rooms in.

Seconds later, the room next door came to life. "So you keep it professional, do you, or is that just for appearance's sake? I'm sure those are adjoining rooms." He chuckled as he pulled a scrap of paper and a pencil out of his glove box. Robby needed to write down everything before the information faded away like the chance of a refreshing breeze on a hot muggy night.

"Okay, names. SSA Jade Monroe and… what the hell was his first name?" Robby rubbed his brow in hopes that it would reboot his memory. It didn't. "Damn it. His last name was DeLeon. That much, I remember." He wrote it down and figured the first name would pop into his head once he stopped trying so hard to think of it. He added the color and make of their vehicle to his notes as well as the name of the hotel and the fact that they were on the second floor and likely in the fifth and sixth rooms from the end of the hall. He looked both ways down the parking lot and at the hotel's windows before getting out of his truck. The coast was clear. He didn't have a reason for doing what he did other than the man and woman were FBI agents. Their agenda was to find out who he was and take him down.

"Sorry, but that's not happening." Robby crept to the passenger side of the Explorer and drove his knife deep into the back tire. "That ought to curb your enthusiasm a bit."

He returned to the truck and drove away but would be back early tomorrow to watch their discovery of the flat tire. At home, there was a trough full of meat he needed to address, and Pete was probably hungry.

Chapter 13

It had been an extremely long day, and I couldn't believe it was still day one of my new position. It seemed like I'd driven to the St. Francis headquarters and met the team a week ago. In reality, it was just twelve hours earlier, but I was beat, and it was about to become a short night.

After a hot shower, I dressed for bed and called Amber. I wanted to update her on the time I had been at the new facility and on what was going on in Louisiana. A half hour of conversation would be my limit since I needed sleep.

I propped up all the bed pillows behind me, grabbed my cell, and made the call. Since we were in the same time zone, it was nine o'clock in both places, and Amber would be awake. I waited as her phone rang in my ear.

"It's about damn time you called."

I chuckled. "How did I know you wouldn't use the standard greeting of 'Hi, Sis, how's it going?'"

She huffed into the phone. "Well, it's nine o'clock, and this is the first time I've heard from you."

"Not so. I sent a text. Anyway, it's the first chance I had to talk, and besides that, I wanted to shower first, get ready for bed, and then call you. I wouldn't have had the energy to shower afterward."

"Fine. You get a pass."

I clicked the remote and channel surfed until I found a local news station. I turned the volume down and redirected my focus to what Amber said she'd made for supper. "That sounds really good."

"It was, and Kate said she loved it too. I'm even taking some to Jack at work tomorrow."

I laughed. "Is that a peace offering for making him feel like chopped liver at Jesse and Hanna's wedding?"

"Yeah, I guess, but I know he was just teasing me."

"Yes, he was, little sister. Jack would never cross that line, and as a matter of fact, he even gave me a wink before he said it."

"Mr. Jokester, huh?"

"Yep. Anyway, my new team seems great, even though I only had a brief meeting with them. I doubt if I was at my desk for a half hour before we had to leave."

"Crazy shit. You FBI agents are constantly on the go. So, what's happening on the ground in Louisiana?"

I groaned as I glanced at the TV screen. The weather forecast for tomorrow showed a hot, sticky, ninety-seven-degree day.

"That bad, huh?"

"What?"

"You just groaned when I asked how it was going in Louisiana."

"Oh, sorry. I saw the weather forecast for tomorrow, but

yeah, the situation here is groanworthy too. Somebody is killing people—" I slapped my hand on the bed. "Damn it!"

"Now what?"

I grabbed the pad and pen that sat alongside the nightstand phone and jotted down a note. "I forgot to ask if they'd determined whether all the bones belonged to women or if some were male bones too."

"Bones? As in without the bodies attached?"

I sighed. "Yeah, that's exactly what I mean, but not entire skeletons. It appears that hunters have been finding piles of human bones while they're out pig hunting."

"Pig hunting? What the hell is that? Don't even tell me they release farm animals into the wild and then hunt them down."

I chuckled. "I won't tell you that because it isn't the case. Apparently, there are wild pigs—tusks and all—that live back in the woods and bayous of Louisiana. What I've been told is that there's a breed of hunting dogs called Louisiana Catahoula Leopard Dogs that hunt wild pigs. They track the pig, surround it, and hold it there until the hunter catches up and shoots it."

"Catawhat?"

"It's the name of the dog breed."

"Humph. Poor pigs. Sounds like they don't have a chance in hell of living through that."

I knew I shouldn't have opened with that since Amber was such an animal lover. "That may be true, but supposedly, if they're wounded, they become very vicious and can attack and kill dogs and humans."

"Good for the pig. They deserve a fighting chance, and I'd do the same thing."

"Okay, okay. I didn't call to talk about wild pigs. Anyway, during the outdoor excursions, the hunters discovered human remains, and the disturbing part is that there wasn't much left, as in muscle. It's like the person's meat was removed and then the bones were disposed of out in the swampland areas."

"That's so disgusting. It's what goes on in slaughterhouses—after the slaughter itself."

"Exactly, like in a butcher shop when they debone meat. Tomorrow, Renz and I are—"

"Hold up. Who?"

I laughed. "I gave my partner a nickname. His full name is Lorenzo, but that's too long. I asked if I could just call him Renz, and he agreed. Anyway, we'll meet up with the sheriff's office and get updates then go out and bang on doors in the areas where the bones were found."

"Are there actually doors to bang on?"

"A few."

"Well, keep me posted and make sure your head is on a swivel."

"Yeah, I was told that some bayou people are odd."

"I was talking about the pigs."

I rolled my eyes and said goodbye. I needed to get a decent night's sleep. With the pillows plumped exactly the way I wanted them, I snuggled in and drifted off.

My phone alarm woke me eight hours later. Even though it was just six o'clock, I felt well-rested. I slipped into the clothes I had on yesterday just to run downstairs and grab a coffee and a sweet roll. I would have breakfast with Renz when I knew for sure he was up.

Back in my room a few minutes later, I turned on the TV and listened to the news as I picked out my clothes for the day. I couldn't bear the thought of wearing long sleeves again and remembered seeing a quick mart attached to the gas station down the street. A stop in there on our way out of town might land me a much-needed can of bug spray.

After finishing my coffee and sweet roll, I changed into clean clothes, brushed my teeth, pulled my hair back into a ponytail, and applied light makeup for the day. A knock on my door told me Renz was ready to go. Just to be sure it was him, I peeked out the peephole and saw nothing but darkness. I laughed since J.T. used to do that too. It had to be a guy thing to cover the peephole with their finger.

I pulled open the door and grinned. "Just so you know, I'm onto you. Every partner I've ever had did that to me, and they were all guys."

Renz snapped his fingers. "Shucks, and here I thought I was an original."

"Nope, no way, no how. Ready to go have breakfast?"

"Sure am. How'd you sleep?"

"Really well. I talked to my sister, Amber, for about a half hour and then called it a night by ten o'clock. I barely remember my head hitting the pillow."

"Same here."

I grabbed my purse, phone, briefcase, and room key. I would put on my badge and gun after leaving the hotel.

Both were safely stashed in my briefcase.

Downstairs, a chef was available to make custom omelets, which I wasn't about to pass up. We filled our plates with choices from the Continental breakfast, along with the omelets, then found a table in the corner of the room, where we could discuss our plans for the day without people overhearing our conversation.

"You remembered the sheet of paper with the other dump site locations, right?"

I nodded then swallowed a bite of raisin toast. "Yep, it's in my briefcase. We forgot to ask if the forensic guys determined if the bones were a mix of male and female remains. I wrote myself a note last night so I wouldn't forget to ask."

"That'd be pretty telling if they all turned out to be female. He could be a predator who targets women because he thinks they're usually trusting and easy prey."

"Uh-huh. We also have to find out if any missing persons reports came in recently for the parish—maybe even the other ones that border Terrebonne Parish too."

"Not a bad idea. We'll check the local area first and then look on VICAP. There could be information of similar crimes that we can track back to Louisiana. About done with that omelet?"

"Yep. Give me five more minutes." I gobbled down the last piece of bacon on my plate and dug into what remained of my omelet.

Chapter 14

We headed down to the car a few minutes later. After Renz clicked the fob, I opened the rear door and set my briefcase on the floor. I mindlessly climbed into the passenger seat at the same time Renz took his spot behind the wheel. He cocked his head and stared at me. "What's wrong?"

"I'm not sure, but something is, unless I'm tipsy this morning."

He chuckled. "Did you pour anything besides coffee into your cup?"

"No, but I feel like I'm sitting lopsided. Look straight out the windshield. Doesn't everything seem tipped my way?"

"Now that you mention it, yeah." Renz climbed out, did a slow walk around the front of the SUV, then came around to my side. I lowered the window.

"I found it." He pointed at the rear of the vehicle.

I stuck out my head. "Can't see shit." I unfastened my belt and climbed out. "How did we get a flat tire? Do you think we ran over something just before we got here and it went flat during the night?"

"Maybe." Renz knelt at the tire. "Or maybe not."

"What do you mean?" I knelt at his side.

He indicated with his finger. "That's a slash if I've ever seen one. If we had run over a nail, a staple, or something like that, it would be lodged in the tire."

I stood and did a three sixty. Nobody appeared to be watching us, and I didn't see cameras on that side of the building. "Now what?"

Renz rolled up his sleeves and scanned the sky. "I need to change the tire before the sun gets on this side of the building. At least now, we're in the shade."

I watched as he jerked the heavy spare from under the cargo area, got the tire jack out, and went to work. He jacked up the Explorer, loosened the lug nuts, and pulled off the flat.

"We'll have to get this plugged somewhere." Within twenty minutes, the new tire was on, and the lug nuts were tightened. Renz put away the tools and looked at his hands. "I better run inside and wash up."

I smiled. "Sure, and I'll stay out here and guard the car."

Luckily, we were off to an early start, so despite the tire mishap, we still arrived at the sheriff's office at eight fifteen. The sheriff, Pat Conway, and several deputies were already milling around. We told the sheriff what had happened, and a concerned look crossed his face.

"There are sketchy people in this neck of the woods. Watch yourselves out there."

Renz said we would take his advice then asked to see the missing persons file that covered the last six months.

Conway swallowed a sip of coffee. "For our parish only? Because if we go into Baton Rouge Parish, the results will be skewed. It's the largest parish in Louisiana."

Renz spoke up. "Yes, only Terrebonne Parish for now. If we have to expand later, we will."

We hovered at the sheriff's back and waited as he logged in to their local reports.

"Okay, during the last six months, we've had seven reports filed, and three of those people were located safe and sound. They were runaways who were luckily tracked down before things took a dark turn."

"And the four others?" I asked.

"Let's see. A seventeen-year-old boy who will be a senior in high school, a married woman who up and vanished from her home, a twenty-one-year-old grocery store cashier, and a twenty-three-year-old young lady who attended cosmetology school and had her own apartment in Raceland."

"And who reported all of them missing? Family members?"

"Mostly people who noticed they were gone."

I gave Renz a side-eyed glance. "And nobody made a big deal of it? Seems like a lot of people to go missing for one parish."

"Our parish covers twenty-one hundred square miles, Agent Monroe, with a bunch of small towns and generations-old family properties scattered about. The owners of those properties are good folks in their own right but don't like law up in their business."

"Then exactly who filed the reports?"

Conway shrugged. "Sometimes it's family, but mostly

workmates or friends. The world is a lot different down here than it is in the north, but as a law enforcement agency, we have to follow up on unusual discoveries like those bones."

I groaned. "So because family doesn't talk to the law, are we going to have guns pointed in our faces when we walk up to a house?"

He shrugged again. "We'll go with you anywhere you need to go, if you like."

I shook my head in utter disbelief. "Zero cooperation from family will probably make finding the killer even tougher."

Conway continued. "I'd focus primarily on the people who filed the reports. You'll get the most cooperation out of them."

I nodded a thanks. "We'll need a printout of those missing people, their addresses, and the names and addresses of the people who filed the reports."

"You bet." Conway tapped the print icon, and the machine behind his desk came to life.

Renz spoke to the sheriff while I looked over the reports. "We'll likely be out all day, but if we don't get anywhere with the locals, I'll check the VICAP database to see if other cases that are similar have come up in Louisiana."

"You do know that there's a lot of voodoo and black magic that goes on in Louisiana, don't you?"

Renz nodded. "I've heard that but have never dealt with situations involving it."

"Black magic or the occult is dark, real dark. It's widely practiced in New Orleans, but in this area, it's becoming even more prevalent. Forbidden Bayou is only a little ways west of town."

My eyes widened. "Forbidden Bayou? What on earth is that?"

"It's where folklore legends come to life. Plenty of spiritual voodoo and animal sacrifices happen back in those swamps. We find areas deep in the bayous where they perform their rituals, do what they do with those damn snakes, and burn their sacrificial animals. We see evidence of animal bones when we stumble across their ceremonial spots, but we've never come across human ones until lately."

I frowned. "We'll keep that in mind."

We started out by driving to the home of the seventeen-year-old high school student whose family lived in Mechanicville. Hopefully, we'd make progress that day, and we planned to ask each family that would talk to us for a sample of their loved one's DNA.

Chapter 15

He thought back to earlier that day when he'd sat in his truck at the end of the hotel parking lot. Robby couldn't wipe the grin off his face. He'd watched as the male agent lugged those tires around, jacked up the SUV, and dirtied his hands.

And as he followed the black Explorer out of town, he sneered. "You haven't seen nothing yet. You get too close and you'll be sorry you ever came to our little community. The Feds don't belong sniffing around Louisiana's business."

Robby would put his enterprise on the back burner for the time being until those agents left town. He needed to keep his eyes on them to see what they thought they knew and what they intended to find out. He couldn't afford to have them ruin everything he'd worked so hard for.

From the sheriff's office, he followed the agents south on Barrow Street then east until they reached Highway 57 and south into Mechanicville.

Hmm... you must be planning to pay Jadon Fish's family a visit. That's a waste of time since his remains are long gone. They were tossed into the swampy muck on the edges of Lake

De Cade, where the gators are plentiful.

Robby waited along the curb and watched as the agents exited their vehicle and approached the modest yellow house. Seconds later, the door opened, and they disappeared inside.

I'm surprised they were allowed in—maybe because the family is considered town folks. Wait until you trespass on bayou people. You'll see what kind of reception you get.

As much as he didn't want to waste the day, Robby knew he would have to follow the agents to find out how many of his victims actually had missing persons reports filed on them.

They're likely looking for information on anyone and everyone who has gone missing, since there's no way in hell they'd have the DNA confirmation yet on any of the bones that were found.

Robby settled in, relaxed, and watched the front door.

Chapter 16

Mrs. Fish wasn't the most welcoming person, especially when we showed her our FBI credentials. She allowed us in, offered us seats, and didn't beat around the bush.

"Tell me why you're here and what you want. I've got people to see and places to go."

Renz passed that one off to me, I assumed because I was a woman and could possibly soften her up.

"Mrs. Fish, your son, Jadon, went missing five and a half months ago. Has he ever contacted you to say he's okay and where he's at?"

She leaned against the wall with her arms crossed tightly over her chest. "No, ma'am."

"And that doesn't concern you?"

She shrugged. "He's a rebellious teenager. I expected as much."

I frowned. "As much as what?"

"I expected him to run off. He was using and selling meth, never went to school, and stayed out all night. He didn't listen to me or his daddy anymore, so I say good riddance to bad apples. If you don't mind the house rules, there's no need to live here."

Her harsh words were startling to hear, but Sheriff Conway had given us fair warning. We wouldn't get a warm welcome from some of the local folks, and I wondered why.

"Ma'am, do you have anything that contains Jadon's DNA? We'd like to add the results to the missing person's report that was filed on him." I wasn't going to tell her that we actually wanted to compare his DNA to the bones we'd found.

"I guess you can take his toothbrush with you. Lord knows he's not coming back for it."

There was a good chance her words were true but not in the way she thought. I asked her to put the toothbrush in a baggie, then we thanked her for the sample. I left my card, and we walked out.

After climbing into the vehicle, I jotted notes on Jadon's paper report. With a sigh, I gave Renz a glance. "How do you want to do this? Interview all four families first and then go back and interview the person who filed each report, or finish up completely with one person before moving on to the next?"

Renz rubbed his cheek. I assumed he was weighing the options. "Who filed the report on Jadon?"

I scanned the sheet. "A woman named Bette Meadows."

Renz frowned. "I wonder who she is?"

"Let's go find out. We have the address."

The home of Bette and Marlin Meadows was a short five blocks away. After we gave two knocks on the door, she welcomed us in.

We exchanged pleasantries then got to the point since we had a full day ahead of us. I took the reins again. "Ma'am, we're here to ask you a few questions about Jadon Fish and why you filed a missing person's report on him."

She scrunched her face. "I did it because his parents don't give a crap about the kid. Alvin, my son, is Jadon's best friend and was worried sick when Jadon up and disappeared. I finally gave up after numerous calls to the sheriff's office to ask if a missing person's report had been filed. Since none had been, I took it upon myself to do it after he'd been gone a week."

"Do you have any idea where Jadon was when he went missing?"

"Alvin invited Jadon over to play video games that night. Jadon agreed and said he was stopping at Grant's grocery store first to pick up snacks. He never came by, never answered his phone, and never was heard from again."

I was taken aback. "So didn't the sheriff's office look at camera footage from the store?"

"Grant's doesn't have outdoor cameras, only indoor ones since shoplifting is a problem. They saw Jadon walk through the aisles, purchase the snacks, and walk out. There wasn't anyone in the store that looked to be following him."

Renz took his turn. "Ma'am, Mrs. Fish said Jadon dealt in and used meth. Do you know anything about that?"

She laughed. "Hell no. That boy was a good kid. If anyone dealt in meth, it was the parents themselves. Jadon worked part-time at that grocery store as a bagger, and it was his only means of income. I probably know more about him than his own mama, and that's pathetic."

"Sounds like you cared about him."

She nodded. "I wish his parents cared as much."

We thanked her, left our cards, and returned to the Explorer.

"I wonder if we're going to hit the same brick walls for the other three missing people too."

Renz shook his head. "Without witnesses to actual abductions, we'll never know who the perp is. We have to follow the plan of collecting DNA samples from each missing person, see if they match any of the bones found, and then really push the family and the missing person's friends about their last known location. The killer has an area he trolls for victims, and we need to find out if that area is somewhere the missing people frequented."

I had to agree. It was imperative to narrow down the possible abduction areas in the enormous parish. My phone rang as we were having that conversation. "Hold that last thought while I get this call." I pulled my phone from my purse and checked the screen. "It's a local number. Must be the sheriff's office." I swiped the green phone icon and answered. "Agent Monroe here." I listened for a second then responded that I was putting him on Speakerphone. It was the sheriff. "Okay, Sheriff Conway, I have Agent DeLeon listening in too. Go ahead with what you started to say."

"Agent DeLeon, I was just telling Agent Monroe that I have a young lady sitting across from me by the name of Gayle Moline who said her sister never came home from the bar Sunday night."

"Keep her there. We'll be back in five minutes." I clicked off the call and fist pumped the air. "This might turn into the lead we desperately need."

We were almost to Houma when the call came in. I was excited to finally speak with somebody about a loved one who had gone missing less than forty-eight hours earlier. Renz parked, and we entered the building.

The deputy behind the counter waved us on. "Sheriff Conway is expecting you. Go ahead."

I nodded a thanks, and we continued down the hallway to the sheriff's private office. The door was standing open, indicating he was expecting us. Inside, a young lady faced him on the guest chair, but she turned when we walked in. Her cute appearance—shoulder-length blond hair, shorts, a tank top, and flip-flops—was marred by her swollen red eyes. I immediately wanted to hug her and say it would be okay, but as a realist, and because of the field I was in, I knew to do otherwise.

The sheriff introduced us and said only that we were there to investigate the disturbing number of people who had gone missing over the last few months. Nobody, not even the press, had been informed of the bone discovery yet.

Conway suggested we talk in their conference room, which had a large table and enough chairs for all of us to sit in. Once inside, I opened my briefcase and pulled out a small recorder to capture the entire conversation while everything was fresh in her mind. As she told us what she knew, I would jot down important points to follow up on.

Renz began the questioning. "First, may I see your

identification? Taking a picture of it is faster than writing everything down."

"Sure." She fumbled with her purse, pulled out her wallet, and slid the laminated card out of the sleeve. She passed it to Renz.

He took the picture and read the information aloud so the recorder could pick it up. After passing the ID back to her, Renz asked Gayle to go ahead with the background information first.

"Carla Moline is my little sister. She's twenty-two years old and works as an assistant at John's Shoe Warehouse." Gayle sucked in a calming breath as she handed a picture of Carla to me, then she smiled through her tears. "She's a cutie, isn't she?"

"Yes, she is, and thank you. I'll make sure you get the picture back after we photocopy it." I gave her a nod to continue.

"We moved here together last year from Chackbay. The town is small—five thousand people—and job opportunities are slim. Our folks live off Dad's disability, and we didn't need to add to their monthly bills by living with them, so we moved south to Houma. It's a much larger city with more opportunity than what we were accustomed to."

I caught up with my notes then asked her to speed ahead to Sunday.

"We just had a casual day, nothing out of the ordinary. We made a batch of chocolate chip cookies after Carla went to the store to buy the ingredients."

"What store was that?"

"Sentry on Main."

My shoulders slumped. My hope for a connection with Grant's grocery store was dashed quickly, and since Mechanicville was three miles away, there would have been no reason for Carla to drive to another town when there were closer stores.

"Okay, and then what?"

"Nothing, really. Straightened up our apartment, watched TV, and talked to our mom on the phone. Carla said she was going to meet our friend Sheila at Bubba Mike's later that night, but since I had to work on Monday, I didn't go along."

"Does Carla have a car?"

Gayle shook her head. "She uses mine at times, but since I had to work yesterday and needed my car, I dropped her off at Bubba Mike's, and she said Sheila would bring her home."

"Do you remember what time you two left?"

Gayle rubbed her forehead. "We watched a reality show, and when that ended, she changed clothes, and I drove her there. I'd say it was around ten fifteen."

"And is Bubba Mike's in Houma?"

"Yes, on the west side of town. I dropped her off, joked about not staying out until five a.m., and then went home. When I got up yesterday morning, she wasn't there. I figured she spent the night with Sheila."

I raised my brows. "And Sheila's last name is?"

"Jackson."

"And she lives in Houma too?"

"Yes, on Bixby Street."

"Then what?"

"Then I went to work at Kyle's Restaurant. I had a double shift yesterday, and when I got home at six o'clock, I assumed she was at work. I texted her a few times but didn't get a response."

"And you weren't alarmed?"

"Not then since they can't have their cell phones out unless they're on break. The phones have to remain in their lockers otherwise."

"So when did you actually begin to worry?"

"Around nine o'clock last night when she didn't come home. Her workmate Dan usually gives her a lift and—"

"Hold up a minute," Renz said. "Dan? Have you spoken with him? And have you spoken with Sheila?"

"Yes to both questions. Dan said she never showed up for work, which completely threw me for a loop, so I called the store to find out if that was true, and it was. Carla never clocked in yesterday. That's when I called Sheila."

Sheriff Conway excused himself for a minute and left the room. We continued with the questions. Moments later, he was back with a carafe of coffee and four Styrofoam cups. I nodded a thanks and poured as Renz asked more about the call to Sheila.

"Sheila told me she felt sick and left the bar around twelve thirty. Carla didn't want to leave yet but swore she would call a rideshare company to take her home."

"Did Sheila say anything about talking to people at the bar? Other patrons, somebody hitting on them or acting too friendly?"

Gayle began to cry and dabbed her cheeks with one of the napkins from the stack Conway had brought in with the coffee. "She said she looked back at Carla before walking out the door and saw a man take her empty seat."

"Hmm… he could have been an innocent patron who wanted to sit down or possibly an opportunist snatching up his chance to start a conversation with Carla," Renz said.

I added my take. "I suppose it could have gone either way. So no ride home and nobody who's a friend or family has spoken with her since twelve thirty Sunday night?"

"That's correct, Agent Monroe."

"Do you know either the Fish or Meadows families?"

She frowned. "No, should I?"

"Not necessarily." I let out a long breath. "Okay, we have to follow up with Sheila. Do you think she's home right now?"

"Um, I don't know. What—"

Renz tipped his wrist. "It's almost noon."

Gayle looked at the ceiling. "She should be unless she's out doing errands. She works from three until eleven at Post Printing. They make a free coffee break type of newspaper that goes out weekly. It has classified ads, store coupons, and those types of things in it."

"And will you be at home later today?" I asked.

"Yes, it's my day off since I did a double yesterday."

"Okay, we're going to follow up with Sheila, go to Bubba Mike's, and then circle back to your place. By the way, do you remember what Carla wore when she went out on Sunday night?"

"I do," Gayle said. "She had just purchased a cute pair of dressy boots, but you couldn't see them with pants on, and it's too hot outside for pants, anyway."

I knew the feeling.

"She decided to put on a little black skirt with a flowery top."

I jotted that down. "What colors were in the top?"

"Peach and coral. Those are her favorite colors."

"Appreciate the information, Gayle. Do you have any idea if Bubba Mike's has cameras?"

She shrugged. "I really don't know."

"Okay, not a problem. We'll check that ourselves and get back to you in a few hours."

Sheriff Conway showed Gayle out while I returned the recorder, pen, and notepad to my briefcase.

"What do you think is the smartest thing to do, Jade?"

I rattled my fingers against the table as I thought. "I think we should put our main focus on Carla Moline. She could still be alive, and her disappearance is recent enough that people may remember seeing her either at the bar Sunday night or somewhere around town yesterday. Let's drop off Jadon's toothbrush at the forensic lab and then go talk to Sheila Jackson and the staff at Bubba Mike's."

Chapter 17

"Now where the hell are they going?" Robby had nearly lost the agents earlier when they'd gunned the Explorer after leaving Mechanicville. They'd returned to the sheriff's office, where they had been inside for at least forty-five minutes, and now they were on the go again. Robby wondered who the young sweet thing was who had walked out a few minutes earlier and if she had anything to do with the agents' sudden return to the sheriff's office.

Staying several car lengths behind the Explorer, Robby followed the agents to an apartment building on Bixby Street, where he saw them park and get out.

"Damn it. There's no way I'll know who they're visiting when it looks to be an eight-unit building." He had no choice but to wait.

Hmm... I am a gutsy kind of guy. I'll give them a few minutes, then I'll take a look at the tenant register myself to see if any name rings a bell.

Robby reached across the seat and pressed the button on the glove box. He pulled out the envelope that contained all the driver's licenses and IDs of his victims and shuffled through them. Nobody he had abducted lived on Bixby Street. He returned the envelope to the glove box, grabbed the door handle, and climbed out of the truck. Acting nonchalant as if he was a visitor to the building wouldn't raise an eyebrow in the slightest, but lurking and sneaking around would. No matter what, he still needed to check the names and do it quickly before the agents came back out. At a fast clip, Robby crossed the street, stepped up to the door, and checked the panel where the buzzers were situated next to each resident's name. He ran his finger down the list, whispering each tenant's name as he did. He didn't recognize a single first or last name. He cursed under his breath, returned to the truck, and took his seat. He had no choice but to wait it out.

A half hour passed before he saw movement at the front door. The agents came out and climbed into the Explorer.

"It's about damn time." Robby waited until they had pulled out onto the street before he made a U-turn then followed a half block behind them. Listening to the radio's music, he tapped his fingers against the steering wheel as he was led to the west side of town. As the neighborhood became familiar, he saw them turn in to the parking lot of Bubba Mike's. "Uh-oh, this isn't good." Robby pressed his palms into his temples. "So they're checking into Carla's disappearance. Even with my ball cap on, the question is, did I ever look directly at the cameras or not?"

Chapter 18

Bubba Mike's wasn't exactly a high-class establishment. It was more of a local joint where a mix of lower-middle-class to bottom-of-the-barrel individuals hung out. Inside, the space was dark, dank, and smelled of skunked beer. The music was louder than any ears should safely tolerate, and the patrons looked like they'd been on weeklong binges. I wondered what the appeal was for people like Carla and Sheila to deliberately go there and consider it a good time.

I took in the scene as my eyes adjusted to the darkened room. "Wow."

Renz cupped his hand against his ear and leaned closer. "What did you say?"

I waved off the comment since my personal opinion wasn't important. What was important was talking to the person in charge and viewing the footage from the camera mounted in the corner that faced the bar. I jerked my head toward the man behind the bar and headed in that direction. Renz followed.

"Excuse me."

The bartender was talking to an older man who had his

head propped up with his folded hands. He was bobbing left to right, and I assumed he'd already had way too many drinks.

I yelled a little louder the second time. "Excuse me!"

A woman to my right butted in. "He ain't going to pay you no attention, honey." She looked me up and down as a cigarette bounced between her lips with every word. "You clearly don't belong here."

"Are you allowed to smoke indoors in Houma?"

She laughed—a definite raspy smoker's laugh. "Who's gonna tell me I can't? You the smoker's police?"

"No, sorry." I jerked my chin at Renz then at the bartender who was intentionally ignoring me. I yelled out, "Put on your tough-guy persona and go talk to him!"

"Sure, no problem."

I watched as Renz cut in on the conversation between the men and pulled out his badge. The bartender grumbled something impossible to hear from my spot then disappeared down a hallway and out of sight.

Renz returned to my side, cupped his hand again, and leaned in. "He's getting the manager."

"Nice work, partner."

Seconds later, a woman with bright-red hair, who looked to be around sixty but was probably forty-five, rounded the bar and set eyes on us. I was sure it was easy enough to pick out the people who wanted to talk to her. Renz, still with his badge in hand, turned it to face her. She didn't say a word but stopped in her tracks and waved for us to follow her. We complied. She waited at the end of the hallway in front of an open door. I glanced at the sign that dangled from a nail. It read Manager Only.

She waved us through and closed the door, where she stood with her hands on her hips while sizing us up. "State or Feds?"

I responded. "Feds, and we need to view your camera footage from Sunday night."

"Do you have a warrant?"

I smiled. "No, but I'd be happy to lock this place down while we get one. I'm sure it won't be too difficult to find plenty of city and state violations in this dump."

She laughed. "Spunky bitch, aren't ya?"

"Damn straight when it's called for."

"Okay, okay, take a chill pill, honey."

I hadn't heard that expression for a good ten years.

"What exactly do you need my camera footage for? Regulars come here every night of the week, and we haven't had any trouble that would cause law enforcement to pay me a visit, especially the Feds."

Renz took his turn. "A young lady went missing Sunday night, and she was last seen here. I couldn't tell you if she was a regular or if she just came by on occasion. She was with a friend who went home around twelve thirty, and then she was on her own. We have no idea what time she left or if she left alone, but the footage would probably give us those answers. How many cameras are in here?"

"Four. Two facing the indoor space where the bar tables are, one by the door facing the bar, and one over the till. None outside."

"We need to see Sunday night's footage from ten p.m. until closing. Let's start with the camera mounted next to the door that faces the bar. I'd assume that everyone who walked through the door would be caught on that camera."

"You'd assume correctly, handsome."

"The name is Agent DeLeon. We know what the missing girl was wearing, so it shouldn't be tough to pick her out. Also, who was tending bar that night?"

"I'd have to check the schedule."

"Okay, can you set up that footage and then check your schedule?"

"I suppose." She deliberately brushed past Renz, chest first, then took a seat at the computer.

I had to hold back my laughter when he looked at me and rolled his eyes.

"There you go. Camera one is up and set for Sunday night beginning at ten o'clock. Just click on the arrow to start it."

We knew full well how to operate forward, back, and pause buttons, but we thanked her, and Renz pointed for me to take the chair. He leaned in at my back. I double-checked the time stamp at the bottom right side of the screen before beginning. Seeing that it was correct, I tapped the forward arrow.

"Hold up a second." Renz had apparently noticed a folding chair behind the door and brought it to my side of the desk. I paused the footage while he got situated.

"Ready?"

He nodded. "Yep. Go ahead."

I tapped the forward arrow again, and we watched what looked to be a large crowd of people in Bubba Mike's.

"Am I missing something? I mean, what's the attraction to this shithole?"

"No clue," Renz said, "but we have to watch the footage closely since it's really dark in there."

"At least we know what Carla was wearing. That has to help."

The bar was crowded, and all we could really see was the backs of people from the waist up as they entered. The camera caught only full bodies who were standing or sitting at the bar or beyond it.

"It's too dark to discern colors, so just watch for a light-haired woman who's wearing a floral-print top."

"Got it. Damn it."

I glanced at Renz. "What?"

"We didn't ask Sheila who got there first, her or Carla."

"That's right. They wouldn't be walking in together. We just have to watch for Carla. Gayle said they left the apartment at ten fifteen." I glanced at the time stamp—10:09. "We still have ten to fifteen minutes before she'd be entering. Do you see Sheila in the crowd anywhere?"

Renz said he didn't, and unfortunately, the footage wasn't the best quality. We continued to watch as people funneled in.

"I bet they're violating the fire code for the number of people that can be in there."

Renz gave me a grin. "You're a stickler for rules, aren't you?"

"Sorry, guess my dad pounded that in our heads as kids." I frowned. "I have gone out on a limb quite a few times, though."

Renz looked surprised. "Really? Care to share?"

I laughed. "Nah. Best to leave the past in the past. I don't want to ruin the stellar opinion the FBI has of me." I pointed at a woman who had just walked up to the bar. "Is that Sheila?"

Renz looked closer at the screen. "Back up a smidge and then pause it."

I did as he said.

"Okay, stop there. Yeah, I think that is Sheila, and she's dead center on the screen. That ought to help identify Carla when she arrives."

"Unless they give up their spots and wander off somewhere else."

"Then the other cameras should catch them."

I checked the time again—10:26. "She should be coming in any second." I focused on the people entering the building as if I had tunnel vision. "There!" I hadn't meant to yell, but I was excited. Renz jumped, causing me to laugh.

"Damn it, girl. You sure are excitable."

I held up my hands with my palms facing him. "Sorry again." I backed up the footage to be one hundred percent certain it was Carla. When she was centered on the screen about five feet inside the building, I paused it. "Okay, floral-patterned top and long blond hair. So far so good. By the time she reaches the bar, we should be able to see if she's wearing a skirt and boots." I grumbled because of the crowd. "Damn it, people, get out of the way." There was finally enough of a clearing to see her skirt, then her hand went up, and she waved. Sheila mirrored the wave. I slapped my hands together. "Yep, that's her." I checked the time—10:45. We were in for a long day of sitting in that stinky building and staring at the computer. "Let's put all of Sunday's footage on a stick. It's something we'll need, anyway, and we're definitely going to have to review it multiple times. Can you go find Red and tell her we're going to copy the recordings from Sunday?"

Renz frowned. "Why me?"

"Really? She has the hots for you. Need I say more?"

Chapter 19

I reviewed parts of the footage again while I waited for Renz to return with Red. When they walked in, it was obvious that she already knew what we wanted. Renz must have explained it to her. She waved me off the chair, took a seat, and tapped a few keys. The footage was being transferred to the stick.

It took a good fifteen minutes to transfer, but when it was done, we thanked her and asked about the bartenders who had been on duty Sunday night.

"It was Chad, Maria, and Todd."

"Great, and who is the guy tending bar right now?"

Red jerked her head toward the door. "That's Chad."

"Humph, Mr. Hospitable. Well, we need to speak with him, so somebody else will have to tend bar while we're doing that."

"I'll send him back." Red left the office.

I smiled at Renz. "You softened her up a bit, I see."

He laughed. "Knock it off. She's definitely not my type."

"Then maybe we should have the discussion about your *type* someday"—I made air quotes around the word *type*—"over a beer."

Renz winked. "Maybe or maybe not."

Seconds later, the door opened, and Chad walked in. "You two need to talk to me about something?"

"Yeah," I said. "Have a seat."

He sat on the desk chair, and we stood. The footage had been queued up to the moment that Carla joined Sheila at the bar.

"Have a look at the footage on the computer. Those two girls came in Sunday night after ten o'clock. The woman on the left went home at twelve thirty, and the one in the flowered top stayed behind. I realize the footage is grainy, but that sure looks like you talking to them from behind the bar."

"Yeah, I worked that night. So what?"

"So you served them numerous times."

"That's my job."

"Exactly. You must have noticed that the woman on the left disappeared after a while and a man took her seat."

"I did notice the ladies weren't together anymore."

"There were three of you working, according to Red."

"Who?"

"The manager."

"Her name is Rita."

I smiled. "Rita or Red, it's all the same to me. Anyway, do you each have an area to bartend?"

He nodded. "I get the left half of the bar, Todd gets the right, and Maria gets the bar tables and fills in during our breaks."

"So you served the same area all night."

"Yeah, mostly."

Renz cracked his knuckles then pocketed his hands. "Do you remember your conversation with those women?"

"Of course not. Unless they're somebody I know, the standard conversation is to ask how they're doing, what they want to drink, and if they need a refill. I don't have time, especially on a busy night, to start up long-winded conversations with anyone."

We hadn't watched all of the footage yet, and the only thing I knew about a man taking Sheila's seat when she left was because she'd told us. I wanted to know what Chad remembered about that. "How about when the woman left and a guy took her place? What did he drink, and was he just sitting there, or did he strike up a conversation with the girl in the flowered top? Can you describe him?"

Chad swatted away my question. "Hell no, I can't describe him. The bar is dark, and there were a good hundred people inside. They came and went. I remember what people order more than I remember the people themselves, though."

The same kind of thing happened to me more times than I cared to admit. I remembered names, addresses, and how people were killed easier than I remembered a friend's birthday.

"Oh yeah, now I remember. The guy ordered a bunch of shots for the lady. I assumed he knew her and maybe it was her birthday or some cause for celebration."

"She let a complete stranger buy her shots?"

"Like I said, I figured they knew each other. He kept buying her girly shots."

"Like what?" I asked.

"Flavored schnapps if I remember correctly. Peach and apple, I think, but she was half in the bag before he sat down. It was obvious she didn't need more alcohol."

Renz took over. "Why didn't you cut her off, then?"

Chad laughed. "You definitely aren't locals. We don't do shit like that here, and once again, I assumed they knew each other and the man was there to be her designated driver."

"What were the ladies drinking for those two hours they were together?"

"The drink I hate more than any other."

I raised a curious brow. "Really? And what was that?"

He cursed. "The gin fizz, and they're a big pain in the ass. You have to shake it forever, and both women were drinking them."

A gin fizz sounded delicious, but we were on duty, and I wasn't about to press my luck with Chad, anyway. "Do you remember how the ladies and the man settled their bills?"

"Cash. On both parts."

I was disappointed but knew a killer—if the man in the bar actually was the killer—would never use a credit card unless it was stolen, and that wouldn't help us.

"Okay, and finally, did the man and woman stay until closing?"

"Nope. I took my last break from one forty-five until two, and when I returned, they were both gone, and other people were sitting in their places."

"So you have no idea if they left together?"

"No, but it's most likely on that footage."

We thanked Chad for his help and left. I was excited to see the footage around the one o'clock hour, and hopefully, we would get a decent shot of the mystery man as he walked out of Bubba Mike's. It was time to head to the sheriff's office, put the stick into my computer, and watch how Sunday night played out.

Chapter 20

Robby wondered what the agents had learned during their hour-long visit in Bubba Mike's bar. There had to be a reason they were in there that long.

Hmm… the only way to learn anything is by going inside and striking up a conversation with an employee and see if they'll tell me anything of value.

Robby looked left and saw the Explorer disappear down the street. He turned in and parked in Bubba Mike's lot. He knew he was taking a risk by going inside, but he needed to know everything the agents knew so he could stay one step ahead of them.

He pulled open the creaky door and entered the dark space. The ball cap, strategically lowered at eyebrow height, would make identifying him difficult. He cozied up to the bar and jerked his chin at the woman who glanced his way.

The redhead strolled over. "What can I do ya for, honey?"

"A tap beer sounds good."

"You got it, sugar."

"What was that about?" Robby pointed his thumb over

his shoulder. "Got some lost officials needing directions?"

She laughed. "You saw them?"

"Couldn't miss them, but they sure as hell don't belong in these parts. I was getting out of my truck when they walked out."

The woman nodded. "Feds, I guess. Come in here all important and shit. Wanted to know about a girl that went missing. They said she was in here on Sunday night and wanted to see my camera footage."

Robby laughed as if it didn't strike a nerve. "Well, they better have showed you a warrant."

"Nope." She lit a cigarette and took a long pull, making the end glow orange. She shook the pack, and another slid out. She offered it to Robby.

"Don't mind if I do. So, no warrant? How do they pull that off?"

"Made some crack about shutting the place down because of code violations if I didn't cooperate."

Robby smirked. "Smart asses think they're hot shit. Bet they stuck their badges in your face too."

"Yep, sure did. Had to end up letting them watch the footage, and then they went ahead and put the entire night on a stick. Guess they wanted to watch it in a more sanitized place." Her voice cracked when she laughed. "That bitch agent really thought she was something, putting out those kinds of threats. We don't take kindly to intimidation tactics."

"No, ma'am, we don't. If she doesn't watch herself, she may end up being gator bait." He laughed loudly, and the woman joined in.

Robby guzzled his beer. "How about another one?"

"You got it, honey, and this one's on the house."

Robby stayed for that last beer then left. He needed to drive past the sheriff's office to see if the Explorer was there. That would tell him the likelihood of the agents being inside and watching all of Sunday night's footage.

Chapter 21

"Can you slow down a bit?" Renz laughed at my enthusiastic pace as I walked to our makeshift office. My laptop was all I needed, and since we knew the general time frame we were looking for, I could set the start time for 1:35 in the morning and go from there. The only thing I cared about was seeing the man's face as he walked out of Bubba Mike's and if he left alone or with Carla. It still wouldn't tell us if he'd abducted her since he could have walked out alone, waited in the shadows for a few minutes, especially if she'd called a rideshare, and then sprung on her and dragged her to his vehicle. After talking to Chad, I doubted that she was even capable of coherently calling for a car, but the killer could have viewed her condition as an opportunity. There was a good chance that he initiated that opportunity by getting her too drunk to turn down his offer of driving her home.

I planned to watch that most important part first, gather what information I could, then review the entire video from the moment Sheila and Carla arrived until the moment Carla left the building.

I jammed the stick into the side of my laptop, opened the video, forwarded the scrubber bar until the time stamp showed 1:35, then patted the chair next to mine.

"Sit down and watch this with me. Two sets of eyes are better than one. I figure by starting the footage ten to fifteen minutes early, we'll see if Carla even got out her phone to call for a ride."

"Good idea." Renz settled in on my right side and gave me a nod. "Go ahead and roll it."

I clicked on the forward arrow and sat within a foot of the screen. Because of the small viewing area and the grainy footage from the bar's dark interior, we had to watch closely. Every minute, I glanced at the time. Finally, I pointed at Chad, who had wiped his hands on a bar rag then walked out of the camera's frame.

"Looks like he's going on his break."

"And I haven't seen Carla take her phone out of her purse at all."

I shook my head. "Look how she's swaying back and forth. She's absolutely wasted. I need to see a straight-on shot of that guy's face since a side view of him wearing a ball cap doesn't help."

"It sure doesn't, and if he is the perp, you know damn well wearing the ball cap was a deliberate act," Renz said. "Sunglasses are the second-best way to hide in plain sight."

I sighed. "True, but at night, that's just stupid and would attract unwanted attention. Plus, as dark as that bar was inside, he'd be walking in blind." I checked the time again—1:53 a.m. "What's the holdup?"

Jabbing the air, Renz pointed. "No holdup. Here we go."

We watched as Carla tried to stand. She nearly tipped over her barstool when she put too much weight against it. The man got up, hooked his arm around her waist, grabbed her purse, and walked her toward the exit.

"Here they come." My finger hovered above the pause symbol.

"Give it a few more seconds. I want their faces as close as possible to the camera before they go off screen."

I waited.

"Okay, now." Renz leaned in. "Damn it. Carla is framed perfectly, but the brim on that guy's hat is blocking his face. Back it up a smidge."

I did as Renz suggested, but it didn't help. It was obvious that the man deliberately kept his head down. He knew full well where the camera was located.

I slapped the table. "Damn him. What does he have to hide unless he's the killer?"

"And notice that his ball cap is black with no logo on it whatsoever. I imagine you can find those anywhere in the United States, and there isn't a single thing that makes it stand out."

I sucked in a slow breath. "Okay, what can we glean from what we have?" I pulled a notebook and a pen from my briefcase. "He has his own vehicle and must have known Carla didn't."

"She probably told him that when Sheila walked out. A stroke of luck for him since there wouldn't be a car left behind and nobody would actually know if Carla disappeared that night or sometime yesterday."

"He has a certain amount of disposable cash since those flavored schnapps shots probably cost three bucks apiece," I added.

"Meaning he likely has a job." Renz frowned. "But would he stay out that late on a Sunday night if he had to work on Monday?"

I shrugged. "Could be a second-shifter or had vacation time, or maybe he planned to call in sick on Monday if he was successful in abducting someone."

"I think we're on the right track. So what else?"

I rubbed my chin as I thought. "He stood taller than Carla, but with his arm around her waist and supporting her, he still wasn't fully upright. I couldn't tell anything about his hair. Couldn't see what he was drinking either and Chad never actually answered that question. He only told us what the guy bought for Carla to drink."

"Yeah, we'll have to contact Chad again."

"The man looked to be of average weight—not heavy or scrawny. Couldn't tell anything of an age to go by since we never saw his face."

Renz huffed. "And we don't have a description to put out to the public either."

I chuckled. "Like the people in these parts are going to help us?" I cocked my head toward the door. "Let's have a talk with Conway. I'm sure everyone knows everyone else around here. There must be a few people who get arrested on a regular basis, and maybe the killer is one of them."

Renz disagreed. "I don't think that's the kind of person we're looking for, Jade. Acts as disturbing as what we're seeing are done by somebody who doesn't want to be found. He's under the radar"—Renz looked out the window—"maybe in the swamps. I'm guessing he's like the nondescript neighbor who ends up murdering twenty people right under everyone's noses."

His comment gave me goose bumps. "So where is he, and how do we find him?"

Renz leaned back in the chair and stared at the ceiling. "Who knows? Maybe he's already found us."

Chapter 22

We had to enlist the help of everyone that Conway could spare from the sheriff's office. We had three other camera angles to review, and with any luck, we would see the face of the man who had spent those last crucial hours with Carla.

Trying to track Carla's cell phone went nowhere. It had likely been turned off Sunday night and was lying at the bottom of a bayou.

Conway called in two other deputies to help. It wasn't much, but we'd take whatever help we could get. Together, we sat in their conference room and talked.

Renz went over what we had—which wasn't a lot.

"We don't know if the man we're checking into is the same person who's dumping the bones, but it would make sense to either drug the victim or, in Carla's case, get her too drunk to resist him. He takes that person back to wherever he lives and does the unthinkable to them. In my opinion, he scouts out his victims. He looks for people who are alone and don't have a car. Tracking down that person's last actions is nearly impossible when their car isn't left behind. That way, nobody knows where or when they were abducted. He disables them and disables their phone or just turns it off and tosses it away. After that, he has free rein to do whatever he likes with his victim."

I took my turn. "He most likely lives alone, and it would be a place where there's enough land and privacy that no amount of yelling would be heard—unless he kills his victim before he takes them home. Either way, he still needs that privacy to butcher and dismember a human body. That takes time."

Deputy Stillman spoke up. "Why on earth is he doing that at all? If he's just a killer, then kill them and dump the whole body. Why are we only finding the bones with a small amount of tissue left on them? What happened to the muscle and organs?"

I grimaced at the direction our conversation was going, but it had to be addressed. "The individual who's committing these acts might be mentally disturbed."

Conway frowned. "And?"

"And he's either eating the victims himself, or he's feeding them to someone or something else." I glanced at the deputies and Conway and was sure I saw their faces go green.

Polsen coughed into his fist. "People really do that?"

"Well, yes, unfortunately, some do, and it could be for a number of reasons. Like I said before, he may be mentally disturbed or—"

Stillman cut in. "Or what?"

Renz answered that question. "Or maybe he just wants to."

I went back to the profile we were putting together before everyone got lost in the image of cannibalism. "He doesn't have a significant other unless they're subservient to him out of fear or they're on board with the murders. Like I said before, he lives somewhere remote where he can kill and dismember without the worry of being seen or heard."

Conway scratched his cheek. "That covers a hell of a lot of area in Louisiana."

I nodded. "Unfortunately, you're right. We assume he comes into Houma to find his victims, meaning he probably lives within a twenty-mile radius of here. He knows the area. He has the confidence or charisma to approach his victims, and he gives the impression of kindness and trustworthiness, so he has to look relatively normal."

"He's a wolf in sheep's clothing," Renz said.

I continued. "His ruse is to help the victims in their time of need. He finds someone who is lost, can't afford a rideshare, is drunk or high, and is definitely alone."

"And then he disables them and goes from there."

I nodded at Stillman. "Exactly."

Renz went on. "We haven't caught a glimpse of his face yet, so we don't have an age to put out there, but we still have to finish watching all the footage. He's of average height—probably under six foot, though—and average weight, one eighty or so. He must have a job. Second shift, we'd assume since he was out late Sunday night. Or he could have taken vacation time or is collecting unemployment. We just don't know yet. We do know that he can afford to go to the bar, buy a young lady a half dozen shots, as well as drinks for himself, and he has a vehicle."

I looked at Conway. "Does anyone around here ring a bell?"

"Sorry, but no, and if he does live out in the swamps, I wouldn't know him. I'm familiar with the in-town troublemakers, and maybe even as far as five miles out, but on a first-name basis, not any farther than that."

"How about hunters?" Renz asked. "Those two who found the latest remains said the work looked like that of a hunter. Any hunting violations lately?"

Conway looked at the deputies. "Check into that, but nothing comes to mind."

Polsen spoke up. "The hunters in these parts all have dogs—packs of them. Those dogs need plenty of room, so most folks live out of town on acreage."

"Those remains were found how far out of town again?" Renz asked.

"Around ten miles," Stillman said.

"Right. So the chances of you knowing people farther out are slim?"

"Yep, unless we've been called out for a disturbance."

"Okay, how about pulling those cases for the last year while we continue looking at the footage?"

Conway stood. "You bet, and we'll let you know when we have that done." He tipped his head toward the door, and the deputies walked out. Conway turned back before closing the door. "Oh, and by the way, Hal called earlier."

I had to think about who Hal was, and Renz spoke up.

"Did Forensics get some news?"

"Yep. The latest dump site results showed that the bones belonged to two individuals—both females. They compared the femurs to the bones that were found last week. They've concluded that the first site contained male bones."

"And Forensics is comparing the DNA on those bones to the toothbrush belonging to Jadon Fish, right?"

"Yep, they're doing that as we speak."

"Good, then we can let the family know if it's confirmed," Renz said.

I muttered under my breath. "If they even care."

It was closing in on six o'clock, and my stomach rumbled. I was sure Renz had to be starving too. I stood and stretched. "We're in for a long night of looking at video footage. How about I run to a fast-food joint and pick up something?"

"That sounds great. I don't care where you go as long as I get a giant burger, a double order of fries, and a large coffee."

"You got it. I'll be back in fifteen minutes or so."

As I crossed the lot to the Explorer, I remembered passing Tony's Burger Shack yesterday on our way to the dump site. It was only a mile or so away and would do just fine. Going through the drive-through would save even more time.

I reached the restaurant at ten after six and saw a line of cars.

Damn it. Must be people picking up dinner after work. Looks like going inside will be faster after all.

I parked, grabbed my purse, and entered the building. As I waited in line, I stared at my options on the meal board mounted on the wall behind the counter.

Chapter 23

"It's about time." Robby turned the key in the ignition and pulled out behind the female agent who had just left the sheriff's office. "Going somewhere alone, are ya? Ballsy move on your part, but I bet that big gun of yours goes everywhere with you. Now, let's see where you're headed." Robby stayed a few car lengths behind the Explorer as the agent drove south. Several minutes later, he saw the right turn signal blink, and she pulled into a fast-food restaurant. "Ah… it's suppertime for you and your sidekick. I'm sure I can use this to my advantage." Robby pulled in and parked three vehicles from the SUV. The agent had already reached the restaurant's door.

After climbing out of the truck, he scurried over to the Explorer and jammed his knife into the front passenger-side tire then casually walked into the restaurant. He scanned the two rows of people standing in line for counter orders but didn't see her. He looked at the patrons seated, but she wasn't among them.

Where the hell did you go? Oh, there you are. Had to pee, did ya?

He waited until she was in line then walked up behind her. Only inches from her head, he inhaled deeply. There was a definite flowery scent to her hair. He couldn't wait to taste her too.

Waiting for the perfect opportunity when someone passed behind him, Robby deliberately bumped into the agent. She turned and frowned.

"Excuse me. I'm so sorry." He pointed at a random person who had already passed. "That idiot wasn't watching where he was going."

She gave him a half smile. "It's fine."

He chuckled, and she looked back again. "Something wrong?"

"No, not at all. Just that you stand out like a sore thumb."

She raised a brow. "I do? In what way?"

He wagged his finger at her clothing. "It's damn near one hundred degrees outside, and you're wearing pants and those short heels. Must be a professional of some sort, but your accent definitely isn't from this neck of the woods. Some kind of traveling salesperson, are ya?"

"Something like that."

He chuckled again. "Or not."

She turned around a third time and looked irritated. "What does that mean?"

He pointed at her exposed sidearm. "You a bounty hunter?"

It was her turn to laugh. "Hardly, but I will say you're observant."

"Can't help it. It isn't often you see a lady wearing a gun, and most people in these parts are more likely to be rifle and shotgun users."

She moved ahead in the row with only two people left in front of her. "Because they hunt wild pigs?"

He was impressed. The agent had done her homework. "Yep, but you can't take that sport lightly. A group of crazed pigs can consume an entire human in under eight minutes."

She wrinkled her face. "So I've heard, and that's too disgusting to imagine."

He needed to step up his game. "If you're interested in those critters, I can be your hunting guide and show you where they live."

She shook her head. "Thanks, but I've already learned what I need to about them from a couple of hunters a few miles south of here."

Robby's ears perked. "Ah, you must mean off Bayou Dularge Road."

She pulled back. "That's exactly where I mean. How would you—"

"Know that? I'm a hunter and know all the hunters in the area. Actually, most men in Louisiana are hunters except maybe the big-city boys."

"Interesting. So do you know Mark LaFleur and Billy Bennett?"

He laughed. "Small world. Yeah, everyone knows them. Great hunters, those two. How would an out-of-towner like you know those boys?"

"I was introduced to them yesterday. Oh, looks like it's

my turn to order. Nice talking to you, um…?"

"Bob. The name is Bob. Just here getting dinner for the family."

"Well, take care, Bob."

"And you too—"

She smiled. "My name is Jade."

He watched as she placed her order, waited, and then walked to the door with it. She looked back and waved. Robby nodded then ordered a cheeseburger and fries.

After he paid for his food, he stood by the window with his bag in hand and looked out. He saw her climb into the Explorer, the lights came on, and she backed up. He would give her a minute then walk out when she realized she was up shit creek. Seconds later, her brake lights flashed, and she climbed out. That was his cue to walk out of the restaurant. After exiting the building, Robby made a sharp right and walked toward his truck. When he heard his name called, he looked over his shoulder.

"Bob, can you help me?"

He turned around and headed her way. "What's wrong?" He heard her cussing as he approached.

"Somebody slashed my tire. The same thing happened yesterday."

"You sure? I mean, kids do stupid things like that all the time, but what are the odds of it happening to you twice?"

She scanned the parking lot. "I don't know, but it's obvious somebody doesn't appreciate me being in Houma."

He waved off the comment. "It's probably just bored kids who are looking for a little excitement. Which tire?"

She rounded the vehicle and pointed at the front right tire. "Yesterday, it was the back one."

Robby scratched his cheek. "Yep, that's as flat as a griddlecake. Pull off to the side, and I'll change it for you."

She shook her head. "Yeah, that won't work. We haven't taken the other flat tire in to be repaired yet."

"Looks like you're in a pickle, then. You'll have to get towed."

"Damn it."

He watched as she dug through her purse then opened the Explorer's door and looked in.

"Well, I'm totally striking out. I left my damn phone in the office."

"How far do you have to go?" He glanced at the position of the camera—there was only one at the drive-through window on that side of the building.

"Just a mile back into town."

He held up his hand. "Let me call the missus and tell her I'll be home in a jiffy. Gotta do my good deed for the day."

"No, really, I can walk a mile. It isn't a big deal."

"But fries taste like crap when they're cold."

"Well, you do have a point. You sure you don't mind? I'd really appreciate it."

"Don't mind one bit. Go ahead and lock up your vehicle." He tipped his head to the left. "I'm right there in that blue pickup."

"Okay, give me a second."

In the truck, Robby made sure none of his victims' IDs were left out. He glanced up as the agent locked her vehicle and crossed the lot to his truck. He reached across the seat and opened the door.

"This is really nice of you, Bob. Did you call your wife?"

"Sure did. She said she was proud of me for helping out a stranded lady." Robby didn't even own a phone, but the agent smiled, and that was all that mattered. He backed out of the spot and turned opposite the drive-through lane, not wanting the camera to catch his vehicle as he went by. He looked left and right at the exit. "Toward town, you said?"

"Yep. Actually, to the sheriff's office."

"Ah, so you're a cop."

"Yes. I'm an FBI agent."

"Impressive. So why are you in town?"

"Can't really say much, just that the locals asked for our help after some recent discoveries."

"And that's how you met Mark and Billy, because they found something while hunting?"

"Yep." She looked across the seat. "And you said you're a hunter?"

Robby stopped at the red light. "Sure am, and probably the best hunter and tracker in Terrebonne Parish. The thing is, are we talking about hunting for game or tracking a murderer? Last I heard, the FBI doesn't involve themselves in unusual animal deaths. That would fall on the shoulders of a wildlife preservation organization."

"Smart guy. Maybe your skills could be useful to us as a consultant in our investigation. Would you be open to that?"

"Absolutely, and I'd consider it my civic duty to help,

but a little compensation goes a long way." He turned right at the main driveway of the sheriff's office and pulled up to the front door.

"Of course, and here's my card. We probably won't be going anywhere until the tires are repaired, but if you can come by here tomorrow, that'd be great. Guess I should have asked if you work during the day."

"Nope. I work the graveyard shift, so I'm available any time after eight in the morning."

"Okay, thanks so much, Bob. Call me in the morning, and we'll arrange a time for you to come in."

"You bet. Nice meeting you, Jade."

She climbed out of the truck with her bag of food and coffees then looked back and smiled before disappearing into the building.

Robby looked at the card she'd given him and flicked it with his fingernail. "Yep, SSA Jade Monroe, you're going to taste mighty fine."

Chapter 24

I pushed open the door with my foot. The bag of burgers and fries was under my arm, and the coffees were in my hands.

"What the hell took so long?" Renz reached for the coffees.

I grumbled, "You aren't even going to believe it." I gave a dirty look to my phone lying next to the computer. "Damn phone. I left it behind."

Renz grinned. "And somehow that's the phone's fault? Give me my food, and then you can explain why you're pissed off."

I groused as I took my seat. "First off, we need to address who's slashing our tires."

"Yeah, remind me to take that spare somewhere tomorrow."

"Well, now we have no way of getting around. Somebody slashed the front right tire while I was in the restaurant."

Renz pulled back. "You can't be serious."

"I'm dead serious, and I couldn't even call a tow truck since I left my phone right there." I pointed at the table.

"Back to the tire slashing. Maybe we need to have a

deputy shadow us while we're in town. It sounds like there's someone who doesn't appreciate the fact that we're in Houma. This could spiral out of control."

"Bob said kids do shit like that, but our vehicle, and twice? Just our luck."

"Who the hell is Bob?" Renz asked.

I chuckled. "Coincidentally, I struck up a conversation with the guy standing in line behind me at the restaurant. He's a local *and* an avid hunter. He even knows those men who discovered the remains yesterday."

Renz took a bite of his cheeseburger and wiggled his finger for me to continue.

"Then I went outside to leave and saw the flat tire. I yelled out to him when he walked out, and then he offered to change the tire once I realized I didn't have my phone."

"And then what?"

"And then I had to tell him we didn't have a spare with air in it. That's when he said kids do things like that. You know, troublemakers with too much free time on their hands. Bob gave me a ride back here. He seems like a nice guy, and there's a chance he could help us by giving us the insight we need to get into the head of the killer."

"Okay, so meanwhile, we have to cut into what we're doing and get the SUV towed and the tires repaired."

"Yeah, let's address that and get back to the videos. Shit!"

Renz shook his head. "Now what?"

"I locked the Explorer."

"Okay, hold on. I'll have Polsen drive me to the

restaurant, we'll meet a tow company there, and—wait, I need to call Conway. What's the name of the restaurant you went to?"

"Tony's Burger Shack."

He smirked. "That's original."

I ate my burger as Renz talked to the sheriff. He hung up within a minute.

"Okay, the impound lot and parish garage is only two blocks away. Conway is having their tow truck meet us at the restaurant, they'll bring the Explorer to the garage, and they'll repair both tires and put one back on. Give me the keys."

"Great idea." I dug in my purse for the keys and handed them to Renz. "So has anything shown up with the perp's face yet?"

"Nah, he got up once and went to the men's room. Kept his head down the entire way and back. We still have camera three to review, though."

"Okay, I'll do that while you're gone."

Renz left the room, and I clicked over to camera three, settled in, and shoved a handful of fries into my mouth. My mind flashed back to Bob. I was hopeful that with his assistance, we would solve the murders before another innocent person went missing.

Chapter 25

Robby returned to Dulac, the town he called home, and searched on the library's computer for information about Mark LaFleur and Billy Bennett. He looked up the various hunting clubs in Terrebonne Parish and found both men listed as board members at HCLL—Hunting Club of Lower Louisiana. After he printed out everything he needed to know, Robby headed home. He would set his plan in motion the next night by stopping in at the hunting club to check it out. His intentions were to befriend both men, invite them to hunt on his property, then make use of those bullets he'd been saving for emergencies.

For now, he needed to feed Pete and the cats. He was sure there was some leftover stew still in the pot on the camp stove.

Once he was home and had fed the pets, Robby grabbed a bottle of beer and looked at the red-stained ground beneath the live oak that he used as his place to restrain and bleed out his prey. Agent Monroe came to mind as he tipped back the bottle and guzzled. She would be a pleasure to deal with, and chances were that she would live far longer than the others.

He planned to gain her trust, show her around the known wild pig habitats, and if more bones were found, say that it likely meant the killer had left them there in hopes that the pigs would polish off all traces of evidence.

Chapter 26

I didn't have any luck with the footage. It was clear that the perp knew where each camera was located throughout the bar and made sure to lower his head every time he faced one.

Renz returned to the office forty-five minutes later with good news. The Explorer was at the impound garage, and the tires were being repaired. It would be ready for us to leave with in less than an hour.

"Did you finish watching the footage?" Renz plopped down on the chair at my side and grunted.

"Yep. Done and useless. We're going to need Carla's DNA to compare to the bones that were found yesterday. It'll either rule out that she was one of those deceased women, or it'll confirm it. Either way, we have to talk to Gayle. It's much later than I had hoped we'd finish up here, and she's probably wondering why we never stopped by. Maybe she can bring something to us rather than us waiting until we have wheels to go over there." I glanced at the wall clock. "It'll be ten o'clock by the time we get out of here."

"I agree." Renz tipped his head toward my phone. "Go ahead and call her."

I made the call and kept it short. Once Gayle was sitting down in person with us, we would explain what we knew up to that point. I asked her to bring either Carla's hairbrush or toothbrush with her and to place the item in a sealed zipper bag.

"So what's the plan for tomorrow?" I took a swig of my cold coffee and wrinkled my nose. "Weird how iced coffee is delicious because it's meant to be cold. Cold coffee that was meant to be hot just doesn't give me that same vibe."

"Yeah, funny how that works. Tomorrow, after we learn the DNA results from Carla, we'll talk to Gayle. After that, we need to continue getting DNA samples from the families of the other missing people. What I'd like to do is match all the bones that were found to people missing from this parish, if that's even possible, and see if they visited any of the same places or knew any of the same people. If the perp is dumping remains of people who lived outside Terrebonne Parish, then I'm at a loss. Dental records won't help if skulls aren't among the bones found and if we don't know who we're looking for."

"What about talking to Bob?"

Renz raised his right brow. "Did you get a last name for this Bob guy?"

"No, sorry, but I gave him my card and told him to call me in the morning. He said he's an expert tracker and hunter. Maybe he can get into the mind of the killer for us."

"Maybe."

My phone buzzed, indicating that a text had come in. Gayle was saying she'd arrived.

"I'll go let her in," Renz said.

We spent the next half hour with Gayle. She'd brought both the hairbrush and toothbrush along in baggies. We explained what we'd seen on the video, and I showed her the only screenshot I'd printed out of the perp's face, which was that sideview with the ball cap on. It was useless for identification purposes, especially in that darkened space, and she said she had no idea who the man was.

"If only Sheila hadn't left early," Gayle said, "maybe that guy wouldn't have taken her seat. It's obvious that he saw an opportunity."

"That's true that he saw an opportunity to talk to a woman and buy her drinks, but it doesn't mean he abducted her." I shrugged. "They walked out at the same time, yet we didn't see Carla use her phone to call a rideshare company prior to that. We'll follow up with companies around town tomorrow." I tapped the screenshot I'd printed out. "We'll also show this picture to Sheila and ask if she remembers seeing the guy in the bar. We'll let you know about the DNA as soon as possible."

Renz walked Gayle out while I called the garage to ask about the Explorer. As I waited for him to return, I packed up our gear for the night, tossed our coffee cups and food wrappers in the trash, and checked my messages. Amber had texted me while I was out, and I would get back to her later from the hotel.

Minutes later, the door opened, and Renz walked in. "What do we know?"

"We know the tires are repaired, and I'm ready for bed."

I grabbed my briefcase and laptop and headed to the door. "They said they were bringing the Explorer over right now."

"Good enough. Let's get out of here. It's been a long day."

"We have to drop off Carla's DNA samples at the forensic lab before we head to the hotel."

He groaned. "Oh, yeah, there's still that."

It was ten thirty by the time we parted ways at our hotel rooms. After a relaxing hot shower, I snuggled up in bed and grabbed my phone. I tapped Amber's name in my contact list and waited as the phone rang on her end. She picked up seconds later.

"Hey, Sis, how's the investigation going?"

"Not getting the leads I was hoping for. It's a slow process, especially when some of the evidence has been out in the elements for weeks or longer. What's going on back home?"

"Same old thing. Unfortunately, we're getting too many calls for domestic violence cases. Jack says it's the times we're living in. There's been a rash of home burglaries too."

"He's probably right. Their way of life is really different down here. Kind of like what happens in Louisiana stays in Louisiana."

"That's creepy, and it would make your investigation tougher."

"Yep, although I met a guy tonight who says he's the best hunter and tracker in these parts. He could be helpful. Also, the sheriff said something that sticks in my craw."

Amber laughed. "Do humans have craws?"

"Who the hell knows, but he mentioned how some people are into black magic in these parts. I mean, I've heard that said about the New Orleans area, so it's possible, then mix that with the reclusive bayou people who want nothing to do with outsiders and—"

"And you have a made-for-TV horror movie."

I laughed. "That would be funny if there wasn't a real possibility of it being true. Anyway, I'm beat, and it's late. I need some sleep, and I bet you do too. I'll catch up with you tomorrow night." I said good night and clicked off the call. After punching my pillow, I turned off the light, sucked in a long breath, and released it slowly. I briefly thought about tomorrow then drifted off.

Chapter 27

The heavy blanket of humidity prevented the swollen wooden door from closing tightly. Robby sat outside in a camp chair and took sips from his first cup of coffee that morning. He thought about last night and his "accidental" meeting with Agent Monroe. It went exactly as he'd hoped, and he reeled her in like a catfish on a line. His motto was to keep his enemies close. He didn't need the first half of that proverb since he didn't have friends to begin with.

I don't have a job either for that matter, but that's something I'll keep close to the vest. That little missy, Jade Monroe, doesn't need to know more about me than I want her to. I'll decide what I tell her, and most of it's going to be bullshit, anyway.

With his cup in hand, Robby walked to the bayou's edge, picked up a broken branch, and tossed it into the murky swamp. A lightning-fast snap of the gator's teeth and the branch disappeared underwater. It bobbed up seconds later.

Fooled you once, shame on me, fooled you twice, shame on you. Dumb reptile, I've fooled you a hundred times.

He walked to the camp stove, lit the burner, and pulled the carton of eggs out of the cooler.

Only two left. Guess I'll be doing some shopping while I'm in town, courtesy of Carla Moline.

With his knife in hand, Robby stabbed a chunk of butter and flicked it into the hot frying pan. The butter melted quickly, then he cracked both eggs and dropped them in. As the whites solidified and sizzled, he pushed them to the side with a spatula. Robby needed room for the slab of meat that was going in next.

After eating, he checked the time—8:42. He had to decide whether to call the agent or not. With his mind made up, Robby drove the short distance into Dulac, made the call, and picked up a few items from the grocery store.

While on the phone, the agent asked if he was willing to work with them, and if he was, would he be able to meet them at the Houma Sheriff's Office at nine thirty. After agreeing, Robby dropped off the groceries, tossed Pete a bone to gnaw on, pocketed his flipper knife, and left.

Grinning as he drove the half-hour distance to Houma, Robby imagined the next few days. Jade Monroe wouldn't see it coming, and the look of sheer panic that would cross her face when she realized she couldn't save herself would be photo worthy.

Too bad I don't have a phone. I'd have an album filled with pictures by now. They'd be something I could look at and reminisce over while I sit outside and enjoy my evening beer.

When he arrived, Robby parked his truck in one of the five visitors' spots at the sheriff's office, got out, and ran his fingers through his four-day-unwashed hair. He took a sniff of each armpit, shook his head, and continued on. Inside the main entrance, he walked to the counter and asked a deputy for Agent Monroe—she was expecting him.

"Your name, sir?"

Shit, I hadn't planned for that.

"Bob Hebert."

Because Hebert was the most common last name in Louisiana—nearly as common as Smith anywhere else—Robby blurted it out. He'd have to stick with the name.

"One moment, Mr. Hebert. I'll see if Agent Monroe is available."

Robby nodded and paced the waiting area.

Seconds later, Jade appeared from the rear hallway with her hand extended. "Bob, it's good to see you again, and thank you. We definitely appreciate any input you can give us." She gave him a wide smile. "And thanks again for the ride last night."

"It's my pleasure to do whatever I can for the FBI, ma'am."

Jade pointed at the other agent in the room. "Bob, this is my partner, SSA Lorenzo DeLeon."

Robby reached out and shook the agent's hand. He'd already knew him by face after following them around town but couldn't remember his first name. "Nice to meet you, sir."

"Likewise, Bob." The agent pointed at the chair that faced them. "Have a seat and tell us about yourself."

Robby pulled out the chair and sat. He wanted to appear

accommodating, informative, and courteous. It would be worth it in the end.

"Name is Bob Hebert—a relatively common surname in this neck of the woods." He chuckled. "Likely a hundred men named Bob Hebert in Terrebonne Parish alone, I'd imagine. Keep to myself, a family man, I'd say. Don't often get in anyone's business, but when Agent Monroe asked if I would consider consulting with you, well, damn, it would be anyone's dream come true to help the FBI."

"What do you do for a living, Bob?" Renz asked.

"I work the graveyard shift as a warehouse stocker in Bobtown, about twenty minutes south of here."

Jade laughed. "That would be funny if you lived in Bobtown. Guess you can't make that stuff up. Right, Bob?"

His face lit up. "No, ma'am, you really can't make that up."

Jade continued. "I've noticed there are a number of cities in the area with unique names. I like that."

Robby nodded. "Yes, ma'am."

She wagged her finger. "Go ahead and call me Jade. People call my mom ma'am, and I'm not quite that old yet."

"Sure thing, if that's what you want."

Renz continued. "So where *do* you live, Bob?"

"Right now, since my wife got laid off, we're staying with her sister and brother-in-law in Woodlawn, just south of Mechanicville. Fallen on hard times for a bit, but we'll get through it."

Jade cut in. "I'm sure we can work out a fifty-dollar-a-day compensation for you."

"That'd be really nice, Jade, and thank you. My sister-in-law will appreciate the help with groceries."

Renz took notes as he asked questions. "Do you know why we're in Houma?"

"Not entirely, sir, but I'd expect it to be a serious situation. Agent Monroe said Mark LaFleur and Billy Bennett showed you something they stumbled across while hunting."

"So you know them?"

"Yes, sir. I've shown most everyone in this parish where the best hunting spots are and how to track wild boars."

"Can you track people too?"

Robby gave him a confident nod. "Yep, I'm the best. All I need is information and a location, and I can tell you when a person was last there, which direction they went, and what means they used to get in and out of the area."

Renz raised a brow. "That could be helpful. Unfortunately, the sites we've been to have been compromised by law enforcement trampling the area."

"Can you give me more information on what I'd be helping with?"

"We were called down here because numerous human bones have been discovered by hunters. They've been found off the beaten path, far back in bayou country, and would probably never have been found if it weren't for the hunters' dogs catching the scent."

"Ah, makes total sense. I'd imagine the dogs made a mess of the area too."

"They had a good start yesterday because the bones were

fresh. The ones found previously may have been weeks old."

"And you're sure they're human and not pig bones?"

"They've been examined by the parish forensic lab, but the skulls confirmed it," Renz said.

Robby grimaced for effect. "Who on earth—"

"That's what we're hoping you can help us find out," Jade said. "We can take you to the locations and show you around. We'd like your opinion of the hunters in the area too. We need to know who exhibits unusual behaviors and may possibly have bad tempers."

"Uh-huh, but why would you think the killer is a hunter? Maybe he's just a local who knows where to hide bodies."

"That's the problem. There were no bodies or even evidence of decomposition. The killer stripped off all the muscle before disposing of the waste, similar to what a butcher would do when separating the cuts of meat from a steer or pig."

"Holy shit. Excuse my French, Jade. I shouldn't talk that way in front of a lady. My mama would have slapped me upside the head for less."

"It's okay. Billy and Mark told us yesterday that we'd be looking for a hunter."

"Or a butcher." Robby stared at Jade, and she looked at Renz.

"That was mentioned, too, and there are butcher shops in the area, right?"

"Yep, plus there are people who have butchering services set up right in their own home."

Renz groused. "Damn it, just another avenue we'll have to follow up on."

Jade spoke up. "The sheriff's office can run point on that, and Conway's deputies can pull permits and do background checks on everyone who butchers meat in the parish." She returned her focus to Robby. "Have you ever heard of anything like this happening before?"

"That the sheriff's office wouldn't already know about?"

"Well, Conway did mention occult practices being prevalent down here."

Robby scratched his chin. That was a gimme and something he could definitely work with. "Ah, I understand what you mean now. Kind of like that dark lifestyle people know of but don't dare talk about."

Jade nodded. "Exactly."

"Yep, I can dig into that further and find out things for you."

"Great. So can you spend the day with us? We'll show you the dump sites first and get your feel of them."

"Sure thing, and I have all day. Just have to be somewhere at seven o'clock tonight."

Jade smiled. "That's perfect, and we'll make sure to wrap up with you by six thirty, then."

Chapter 28

"Looks like you got your tires fixed." Robby climbed into the passenger seat of the Explorer. "That's got to be a real pain in the butt. Darn kids these days. I've taught my kids better than that."

"So, how many kids do you have, Bob, and how old are they?"

He looked over his shoulder at Jade. "Two. Brent is sixteen, and Leanna is twelve. They're good kids, and that's all on their mama. She cracks the whip when need be."

Renz redirected back to the first comment. "So, you don't think somebody is targeting us specifically because we're outsiders?"

"Who would know that unless you've been prodding folks? People around here don't take kindly to that type of treatment."

"The only people who seemed irritated with us were the manager and one bartender at Bubba Mike's," Jade said.

"Have you ever been there, to Bubba Mike's?" Renz asked.

Robby looked at Renz. "No, sir. I'm not a drinking man,

and my wife would have me by the short hairs if she ever caught wind that I was in a bar."

Jade laughed. "Sounds like she cracks the whip on you too."

"Yep, she sure does. So where is this dump site?"

"Ten miles out of town, so just a few more miles beyond Theriot."

"On Bayou Dularge Road?"

Jade leaned forward. "Yes, off a gravel path that used to be a road, I guess. It goes back to the water. Why?"

"Not a good sign. Nope, not a good sign at all."

"Are you going to tell us more or keep it to yourself?"

Jade frowned. "Renz."

Robby let out a longer than necessary sigh. "Sorry. It's just one of the stories I heard growing up about that area, back there by the water. Very disturbing things. You know—"

"You mean voodoo, black magic stuff?" Jade asked.

"Well, according to my mama"—Robby made the sign of the cross—"God rest her soul, there was a crazy woman who lived back there. Had a stilt house on the water that was burned to the ground after the police found the bits and pieces of what remained of her family. She'd killed her husband and kids—all of them. In her mumblings to police, she said something about how the spirits would torture her soul if she didn't do it. She shot every last one of them and tossed them in the bayou for the gators to devour." Robby shook his head. "I heard there were bones all over the place back there. That woman went completely off her rocker, some said. I guess she couldn't handle being poor with a drunk for a husband and too many kids that she couldn't feed. Others said she talked one too many times to Lakita Blanc."

Jade's eyes widened. "Who the hell is Lakita Blanc?"

"A soothsayer who used to live in these parts. She passed years back, thank God. She's the one who told the woman—Olivia Broussard—that when she died, her ghost would haunt the area forever if she didn't commit the deeds. Her kids were suffering from hunger, and the old man needed to die, anyway, because he was just that mean, and if Olivia didn't do it, she'd never rest in peace. Some say they've seen her wandering the edges of the bayou, looking for the bodies of her babies."

"Who would know that if nobody goes back there?" Jade asked.

"Hunters, I guess, although a gun can't do much good against a ghost."

"Sounds like an urban legend to me," Renz said.

"Well, I don't know the truth either way, just repeating what the locals have said over the years, but I'd almost want to be sprinkled with holy water before going back there. Those kinds of stories are told far and wide in these parts."

"So what exactly are you saying? You don't want to help us?" Renz asked.

Robby held up his hands. "No, no, no. I made a commitment." He looked out the window as they slowed down. "And at least it's daylight."

Renz turned onto the gravel path that Robby was plenty familiar with, and the brush that had taken over what used to be a driveway scraped the sides of the Explorer.

Robby knew Jade believed his story, but convincing the other agent would be tougher. He'd have to win his trust too—somehow. Planting evidence wouldn't be the worst idea. No matter what, he planned to have fun with those two big-city FBI idiots, and in the end, they'd be dinner for the gators. At least Lorenzo DeLeon would.

"You know this gravel path used to be the driveway to the Broussard home."

"I thought it was an overgrown road," Jade said.

"Nope. It dead-ends at the water."

"So you've been back here?" Renz asked as he stopped in the road and parked.

"Yep, back a number of years ago, I'd hunt here, just never alone. That story gets in my head and kind of spooks me. Anyway, it looks like we're as far as we can go." Robby opened the passenger door and stepped out.

Jade climbed out on the same side, and Renz rounded the front of the vehicle.

"Where to?" Robby asked and then sniffed the air. "Never mind, I know where to go." He cut through the brush on the path that the deputies and forensic team had created. It was worn down to the bare ground from people tracking in and out. "There's no way I can find anything back here as far as clues the killer might have left behind. The scene is obviously contaminated beyond hope." He continued on for a hundred feet then stopped. "This is it, right?" He sniffed the air. "Yep, I smell dogs, pigs, and human remains along with body sweat."

"You can smell all that?" Jade asked.

"You bet. That's what trackers do, as well as look for signs like broken twigs, snagged cloth, shoeprints, anything that doesn't belong out here in nature. As far as the scents go, the dogs and pigs urinate and leave their mark. People, they just sweat. I'd be able to tell you more if the scene hadn't been trampled. I imagine there were a half dozen vehicles back here too?"

"Yeah, there were."

"So nobody checked for tire prints?"

"Not to our knowledge, but Forensics—"

Robby waved off Renz's comment. "They're only looking at the obvious, not the things that are out of place in nature." Robby knelt, picked up a handful of soil, and sifted it through his fingers. "More bugs and maggots than what would normally be back here. There were bones and pieces of skin or tissue, you said?"

Jade nodded. "Yes, that's right."

"Did you take pictures, too, or just the forensic guys?"

"I did, but I'm sure they aren't nearly as good as the professional-grade pictures they took," Jade said.

"Then it would be helpful to see their photos."

"I'll see what I can do." Jade made the call to the forensic lab and asked if some of the photos could be emailed to her. She hung up seconds later and said she would have the pictures soon. "Let's head back to the sheriff's office. We'll have the pictures by then, and we can view them on my computer."

Robby turned and started walking off. "If the forensic

team has good equipment in their lab, they should be able to determine what kind of knife was used to remove the meat from the bone."

"Meat?" Jade cringed. "That doesn't sound like we're talking about human remains—it's more like something you'd eat."

"Okay, then, I'll call it muscle and tissue, but in the end, it's all the same. Somebody removed the"—he made air quotes—"*muscle and tissue* from the bones for a reason, and consumption is the only explanation I can think of."

They were back at the sheriff's office twenty minutes later and took seats around Jade's computer. She enlarged the photos in the attachment Forensics had sent over, then moved the laptop to sit in front of Robby.

He scooted in closer to the screen. "Are these images enlarged as much as possible?"

"Just hit the plus icon. It'll make them as big as they get."

Robby went through the nine photos. "I can't tell you anything, really, since I'm looking at a one-dimensional photo. The depth and length of the cuts and scrapes would tell you the size of the knife and the thickness of the blade. We'd know if it was a hunting knife or a butcher's knife."

Jade raised a brow. "You can tell the difference?"

"A hunter would know, but I can't say with any certainty that a forensic tech could tell the difference. Did the sheriff get back to you about the butchers in the area? I might know if some of them are iffy characters once I see their names."

Renz stood. "I'll go ask."

Jade and Robby sat quietly while Renz was gone, then Jade spoke up. "If there are so many waterways in the area that are teeming with alligators, then why wouldn't the killer just toss the remains in the water and let nature take its course? I mean, why risk being seen dumping the bones back in hunting grounds?"

Robby scratched his head as if puzzled by the question. "That's a good question, and I have two possible answers."

"Go ahead."

"He assumed the wild pigs would eat the evidence and it would never be discovered."

"And the other reason?"

"He lives near the water, where gators are plentiful."

"Then that seems like the perfect place to get rid of the remains."

Robby shook his head. "Nope, it's the worst place. You know how signs are posted in zoos, parks, lagoons, and so on about not feeding wild animals?"

Jade nodded. "Yes, I've seen them."

"Well, it's the same concept. Feed a gator all the time and they'll keep coming around. Pretty soon, they'll be waiting on your doorstep for food. That's when the person feeding them becomes the food."

"Geez, I never thought of that."

Renz returned with several sheets of paper.

"What did you find out?" Robby asked.

"Here, take a look. There are three butchers in the parish with police records. They vary from petty theft to battery and finally to serving time. Do you know any of them?"

Robby scanned each sheet then jabbed the first one. "I'm somewhat familiar with Tommy French, but he's not the killer."

"How do you know?"

"He's too much of a lightweight. He wouldn't have the strength to overtake a ten-year-old kid let alone an adult, even if it was a female. Plus, his wife does most of the butchering work. He's too squeamish. He puts the cuts in the display cooler, wraps the meat, and rings up the purchase."

"So you're saying his wife does all the heavy lifting?" Renz asked.

"Yep. That's exactly what I'm saying."

"And you don't know the other two?"

"I'm afraid not."

Renz tapped his pen against the table while staring at Robby. "Okay, I think that's all we need for today. Why don't you go ahead and spend the afternoon with your family? You can put together a list for us of locals who you think could be suspicious individuals. You know, people who kind of stay off the grid that law enforcement wouldn't necessarily know of."

"Yep, I know a dozen or so people who fit that description."

"Good. Then we'll review that list tomorrow and see if anything shakes out."

Robby stood, slapped his hands together, and said goodbye. He had to make plans for his introduction to Billy and Mark, anyway.

He was back home just outside Dulac an hour later. Robby had called the elite HCLL and said he wanted to become a member. That night, he would complete the paperwork and attend the new members' welcome meeting hosted by the staff of the hunting club. Two of those members were Mark LaFleur and Billy Bennett, the men he was most interested in getting to know.

Chapter 29

Robby arrived at the hunting club at six forty-five and stepped up to the counter and asked for a membership application. After being handed the sheet on a clipboard, he took a seat along with several other people in the lounge area and filled in the information.

At seven o'clock, the new attendees moved to the meeting room, where they watched a video showing all the benefits that the club offered. There were biweekly meetings, indoor and outdoor ranges, private training, a shooting store and gift shop, and a bar and restaurant. After the video, Mark LaFleur stepped up to the podium, welcomed the new members, and took questions. By eight o'clock, the room where a meet and greet cocktail party was set to take place had filled with existing members. It was scheduled to end at ten o'clock. By then, Robby was certain he would have Billy Bennett and Mark LaFleur in his back pocket.

People mingled and introduced themselves. Robby knew Billy's face only by his picture on the website, and he scanned the room for him while enjoying hors d'oeuvres and wine.

Ah, there he is. Time to let him know what a lucky guy he is to meet me, and I'll be repeating my credentials to Mark LaFleur, too, before the night is over.

Robby approached Billy Bennett and reached out to shake his hand. "Billy Bennett?"

"Yes, that's me, and you are?"

"Robert Williams, a new member of this group. Pleasure to make your acquaintance. I have a question that was never asked during the question and answer session."

"Shoot."

They both laughed. "Good one."

Billy nodded, clearly pleased with himself. "I'll admit, I use that often. So, what's your question?"

"It wasn't mentioned on the video, so I was just wondering if the club owns any hunting land that's used exclusively for members."

Billy scratched his cheek. "Unfortunately not. Most of our members are city boys who don't own land of their own and either shoot at the range, enjoy the amenities here at the club, or go out on public land to shoot."

"Where I bet a lot of other members go."

"Well, that is true. It seems to scare away the wild pigs, so we have to keep going deeper and deeper into bayou country to find land that isn't so populated."

"Maybe I can help out with that—essentially a barter system. If my membership fees are waived, I'll allow people to hunt on my property."

Mark strolled up on the conversation, and Billy made the introductions. "Mark LaFleur, this is Robert Williams, and it sounds like he has an interesting proposition for the club."

Mark appeared to be intrigued. "Really? And what's that?"

"Let me explain it to you over another glass of wine."

The three men found seats at a corner table in the bar.

"Now, what is it you have to offer, Mr. Williams?"

"Just call me Rob. Most of my friends do."

"Okay, Rob, go ahead."

"Well, I own two hundred acres of pristine land that backs up to the bayous around Dulac."

Mark grunted. "That's a half hour away."

"Yes, it is, and that's why it's still good hunting land. All your good ol' boys who belong to this club and hunt around Houma have wiped out a lot of the pig population, plus the fact that the space is overpopulated with hunters doesn't help matters." Robby lowered his voice to just above a whisper. "Word has it that you two discovered something Monday off Bayou Dularge Road."

Billy pulled back. "How in the hell did you hear about that?"

Robby shrugged. "News travels fast. That alone is going to give hunters pause. You never know what kind of lunatic might be out there with a gun, except he isn't hunting pigs—he's hunting people."

"We can't take your proposal to the board until we see your property."

"And I wouldn't expect anything less. When can you fellas come out? We can even get a few hours of hunting in, too, if you'd like. No need to bring the dogs either. I know exactly where the pigs are."

Billy looked at Mark. "What do you say? Tomorrow morning works for me."

"Yeah, me too. We'll have you walk us around your property, maybe even take a few shots if we spot some pigs, and then make a decision."

"Great. I guarantee you it'll be a blast."

They chuckled at his choice of words.

Robby grabbed a pen and a piece of paper from the bartender. "Let me give you my address."

Chapter 30

Robby had been up since the crack of dawn. He cursed the fact that he had to drive into town to leave Agent Monroe a message saying he wouldn't be available until noon. He had far more exciting and necessary things to take care of that morning. Even though he'd given the agents false information about every aspect of his life, the fact that Billy and Mark had told them they should investigate hunters would eventually lead to him. That part of his life was true—he was an expert hunter and tracker. Even though he wasn't known by many, the people who did know him could eventually lead law enforcement to his doorstep.

With a travel mug of coffee in hand, Robby climbed into his truck and took Four Point Road to the edge of Dulac.

Maybe I'll get a cell phone someday, but that just gives people more opportunity to snoop into my business.

He stopped at the southernmost gas station and used the pay phone there to make the call to Agent Monroe. After hanging up, he immediately turned around and headed home. He had to set the trap for his guests, who would arrive in less than two hours.

He sorted through the supplies he needed and dropped everything into a burlap bag. With the bag in hand, he headed out on foot, and fifteen minutes later, he reached the location he'd chosen deep in the shaded underbrush. With multiple nesting areas, it was a hot spot for wild hogs, and as he approached, he made as much noise as possible to scare them away.

Wild pigs were more active at night but did occasionally come out during the day in search of food. Bringing the men back to the pigs' nesting ground and suggesting they get off a shot would keep them distracted long enough for Robby to do what he needed to do. It was necessary to keep his lifestyle running smoothly, like it had been before those FBI agents waltzed into town.

He chose two large trees that were a good ten feet apart and drove nails deep into the trunks. Using the claw hammer, he bent the nails over to act as loops to slip the ropes through. He wasn't about to risk the men freeing themselves by sliding their arms up and down to create enough friction to break the ropes. The men seemed savvy and likely had a keen knowledge of survival techniques.

With his supplies well-hidden and the pigs at bay, Robby returned to the shack and walked the immediate area. He didn't want to be surprised by something that still remained in the burn pit or near the tree that he'd tied his victims to. At the base of that tree, he kicked dirt over Carla's several-day-old bloodstain on the ground. After pulling his camp chair back to the shack, Robby straightened up the yard and tossed empty beer bottles in the trash can.

He had to think of a believable story to explain the condition of his living quarters. The night before, Robby had presented himself as someone who could afford the five-thousand-dollar-a-year membership into the elite club but who was willing to trade the expensive fee for "members only" hunting privileges on his virgin property.

I'll tell them that this is my hunting shack and I come out here several times a month to enjoy the sport and to have some outdoor peace and quiet. Gotta have that "me" time.

His blue truck, which had seen better days, would be covered with a tarp. Robby was a great storyteller who could spin a yarn in seconds flat, and he would do so as he showed Billy and Mark around.

He gave the property one more look, and all was well. He took a seat on a camp chair and watched the driveway. Soon, he expected to hear gravel crunching under tires, and what followed would make his heart pound with excitement.

Robby tipped his wrist and checked the time—9:02. They would be there any second. When he heard a distant sound, he cocked his ear. It was one he recognized from his own truck making its way down the driveway. He rubbed his hands together with enthusiasm. It was just a matter of time.

Less than a minute from the first sound he'd heard, Robby saw the flash of red between the tree cover—a truck was coming his way. He stood and moved the chair from the driveway then waved at the slowing truck. He gave them a thumbs-up, and the driver stopped. Billy was behind the wheel.

That's a nice truck, and I could use a replacement.

The men opened the doors and stepped down off the running boards.

"Damn, this place is really off the beaten path. Surprised my GPS even recognized how to get here." Billy extended his hand and shook Robby's.

Robby reminded them, "The only way to have untouched hunting ground *is* to be off the beaten path, plus I like the privacy."

Mark looked from left to right. "You don't live here, do you?"

"Nope. It's my man's playground, nothing more. Like to get away from the old lady now and then, if you know what I mean."

Billy huffed. "I definitely know what you mean. Damn women sometimes. The wife and I already had a fight this morning before I left."

Robby shook his head. It would be a problem if Billy had told his wife where he was going. "She probably thinks you stormed off because of the fight."

"Nah, I told her that I had a business opportunity to check out this morning, but she wanted me to mow the lawn." He pointed at Mark. "He's the smart one and has remained single all these years."

Robby grinned then continued on. "Well, as you noticed, I have a long driveway, so I can clear the edges a bit to make room for angled parking."

"How many acres did you say you have back here?" Mark asked.

"Two hundred give or take."

The guys could have no idea that Robby already leased his land for hunting purposes to make a little extra money. Between that and the cash he took from his victims, he had enough to get by.

"And it's full of wild boar?"

"Yep, teeming with them, and plenty more than I'll ever need. Why don't you grab your rifles, and we'll head out. I'll show you one of their current nesting spots."

"I didn't bring mine," Billy said. "My freezer is already filled with game, plus, the wife would've had a fit if she'd seen me walk out with my rifle. I did that a couple of days ago, and she nearly strangled me since I've been promising to cut the grass for two weeks now. What the hell? It's only a foot tall."

They had a good laugh, then Robby addressed Mark. "Okay, then, how about you?"

"Yep, brought my thirty-thirty along."

"Good deal, so let's head into the woods. I have somewhere to be in a few hours."

Robby led the way single file through the brush just fifty feet from the water's edge.

Mark pointed. "Don't the gators ever get the pigs?"

"Sure they do when the hogs go down to drink. There's plenty of both in this area, so you always have to be on guard and carry a gun."

Billy looked at Robby. "Then where's yours?"

"I didn't bring it since Mark has one. That way, I don't jump the gun and fire." He chuckled at his play on words. "Anyway,

I want you to take the shot if there's an opportunity."

"Hell yeah, I'll take the shot," Mark said.

The morning couldn't get much better. Only one man had a gun, and that made Robby's job a lot easier. He would have to take careful aim and hit Mark in the shoulder so he wouldn't be able to fire the rifle.

"You left- or right-handed, Mark?" he asked as they followed him into the woods.

"Right-handed."

"Okay. I just want to stay out of your way when you get ready to shoot." Mark's answer told Robby which shoulder to hit. He would have to disable both of them quickly before Billy had a chance to pick up Mark's rifle and shoot back.

They were closing in on the nesting ground. Robby wasn't sure that any of the pigs had come back yet after scaring them away earlier.

"We're getting close, so keep your eyes peeled." He pointed in the direction of the bayou. "They've created a trail between here and the water's edge. You might want to give it a look while I take a piss."

"Yeah, sure. Good idea."

Robby headed to the spot where he'd left the bag. He looked back and saw the men walking the trail. He opened the bag, pulled out the 9mm Glock he'd stolen last year, and quietly racked a round into the chamber. When the moment was right, he would have to take good aim since he wasn't quite ready for the men to die. He wanted to enjoy seeing what the pigs would do to them once the men were tied to trees and bleeding in the nesting area of a half dozen wild boars.

He needed to be within thirty feet of Mark to get an accurate shoulder shot, especially in the thick tree cover. Missing Mark's head or lungs gave Robby only an eight-inch circumference to work with. He had to take an accurate and steady shot.

He called out to let them know he was coming. "See anything yet?" When he finally caught sight of them, he noticed that Billy was in the back as they walked single file. That wouldn't work.

"Mark, since you have the gun, head right a bit. You'll have to scare them out of that thick undergrowth. Billy, stay on the trail so I can see you."

"Yep, got it."

The setup was working to perfection. The men parted ways, a good six feet of separation between them. Robby lifted the Glock, put eyes on Mark's shoulder, and squeezed the trigger. The ear-piercing crack echoed loudly, and they were soon surrounded by the sounds of animals running frantically through the woods.

Mark let out a grunt then a yell as he dropped his rifle. Billy spun to see the barrel of Robby's Glock pointed at his own kneecap.

"What the hell, dude! What in God's name are you doing?"

"It's my own pig-versus-man experiment." Robby pulled the trigger and dropped Billy to the ground, destroying his knee, and then immediately walked over to

Mark and grabbed the rifle. "I'll take this weight off your shoulders, literally." In a flash, Robby clubbed Mark in the head with the stock of the rifle, then he went directly to Billy and did the same thing. He rubbed his hands together. "Now the fun is about to begin."

After grabbing Mark by the ankles, Robby dragged him to the path then another hundred feet to the tree where he would be tied. Since Mark had two good legs and could run when he woke up, it was imperative to secure him first. Billy wouldn't be able to stand with a shattered kneecap, so he wasn't going anywhere.

Robby took the goody bag to the tree, pulled out the rope, and began tying it around Mark's hands. He slipped the ends of the rope through the nails on either side of the tree and pulled them tight as he lifted Mark to a standing position, then he secured the rope ends to each other. He covered the knotted ropes around Mark's wrists with multiple layers of duct tape just to be on the safe side, then he did the same to the rope behind the tree. When that was complete, he knotted ropes around Mark's ankles and repeated the process. The final step was to cover Mark's mouth with a length of duct tape wrapped around his head so he couldn't rub it off against his shoulder, even though nobody in a five-mile radius would hear his cries for help.

With Mark out of the way, Robby checked the time, 10:17, and he was right on schedule. Billy was next, and from his moaning, it appeared that he was waking up. Robby would have to hurry or clock him in the head again if he regained consciousness.

Robby grabbed Billy by the ankles and yanked him. He heard bone scraping against bone and felt the left leg give way. It probably wasn't held together by much more than a few tendons. Robby chuckled as he imagined being forced to stand on a broken leg. He was sure the shredded muscle and bone mixed with blood would go a long way with the pigs, plus a torn-up leg was far easier to reach and chew on than a shoulder that had been shot.

As Robby tied the ropes to Billy's wrists and hoisted him against the tree, Billy's screams and thrashing told Robby his guest was wide-awake.

"Stop fighting me! The more you fight, the more it's going to hurt."

"You son of a bitch! What kind of lunatic are you? I have a wife and kids at home!"

"Who are probably better off without you. You so much as admitted that having a wife was a pain in the ass. I bet she'll be thrilled that you're gone, but if she isn't, I'll be more than happy to ease her pain."

Billy spat in Robby's face, an act that was met with a punch to the temple. Billy passed out again.

"Good, now maybe I can get something accomplished."

With a few more twists of the rope and a half dozen more knots, he guaranteed that Billy Bennett wasn't going anywhere. Robby wiped the blood and dirt on his pants, checked his work once more, then emptied both men's pockets. The phones would be shut down and tossed in the bayou, and the wallets would be relieved of their cash. Everything else except the truck keys would be burned in the firepit. Robby had to figure out what to do with that truck. A paint job and a swap with his own plates would suffice until he could change them up again with plates from a different parish.

But first, he had to get cleaned up and head to Houma, where the FBI team was expecting him.

He picked up his bag and Mark's rifle, said goodbye to the head-bobbing men, and made his way through the brush to the shack. As he walked, he reminded himself to call the state office later and suspend the hunting on his property for a few weeks, and he still had to compile that list of names for the FBI.

Chapter 31

"I don't know if Bob has anything to offer us, Jade. I think he's just a blowhard who's looking to make a few bucks on the side."

I shook my head. "I don't have an opinion one way or the other yet. We've only given him a half day to work with us, and he's compiling that list of sketchy characters who law enforcement wouldn't necessarily know, the ones who live off the grid."

Renz rubbed his forehead. "There is that. We'll take a look at that list, see if they have a record, and interview the people who are still in the area. Guess we'll have to see what pops."

I frowned. "What's going to pop if law enforcement doesn't know they exist? That would probably go for the wackadoodle black magic people too. Kind of like the darkest dark web. If you don't know about it, you wouldn't have a clue to the extremely disturbing things that go on behind that black curtain of crime."

"I suppose you're right."

I nodded. "Let's give him a few days. We're committed

to being here a week, so let's make the best use of that time."

"And the best use of it is with Bob Hebert?"

I shrugged. "Just saying." I checked the time, and Bob was due to show up any minute. I poured myself a fresh cup of coffee just as Conway gave the half-opened door a knock. Renz waved him in.

"I have news."

Renz pointed at an available chair. "Let's hear it."

"Forensics got back to me. A match came in for a young lady who was identified by the dental records supplied by her mom. She'd been missing for three months. Her bones were found at the second dump site."

"And yesterday's dump site was number three?"

"Of the locations we know of, yes. Also, Carla Moline's DNA doesn't match any of the bones found so far."

"Wow. That's not what I was expecting to hear," I said. "So what the hell happened to her?"

Conway shook his head. "No clue. Maybe that guy who was with her at Bubba Mike's actually did abduct her but didn't kill her. He could be holding her somewhere."

"I called the rideshare companies in the area and nobody made a pickup at Bubba Mike's on Sunday night after eleven o'clock," I said.

"Damn. That just added another twist to this case."

Renz huffed and gave Conway a glance. "That's if the cases are even related."

Conway groaned. "Any leads coming in yet?"

"Nope, but we are working with Bob Hebert."

"Not familiar with the name."

"He's living in Woodlawn with extended family for now. Guess he's a good tracker and hunter and may know of a few people who live on the sketchier side of the tracks."

Conway rolled his eyes. "And God knows there's plenty of those folks who have moved to this area from the big cities."

Seconds later, Bob walked in. Renz introduced him to the sheriff, they exchanged a handshake, then Conway left.

"Sorry I'm a few minutes late. Had to gas up on my way into town." He reached into his pockets, pulled out two Snickers bars, and handed them to me.

I let out a surprised laugh. "What the hell is this?" If I was right, it looked like a bright-red blush covered Bob's cheeks.

"Nothing, really. Just noticed the wrappers in your trash can yesterday were all from Snickers bars. Like I said, I'm a good tracker, and I notice everything, whether it's out in the wild or in a trash can."

I joked with him. "Damn it, Bob, I think you're in the wrong profession. Maybe you should think about becoming a cop."

He swatted the air and chuckled. "That's probably the nicest compliment I've ever gotten, Jade."

I had my doubts, but it was sweet of him to say.

Bob took a seat across from me, the same chair he sat in yesterday. "So, have you had any success yet?"

Renz spoke up. "The sheriff just gave us some unexpected news."

"Good news, I hope." Bob looked from me to Renz and waited.

"A girl was reported missing a few days back by her sister. We'd assumed—"

"That some of those bones were hers?"

"Yes, but Forensics said they weren't. They compared her DNA to the two sets of bones at yesterday's site and the bones from an older site—no match."

"Have you had luck identifying any of the victims?"

"A match did come in overnight to a young lady who went missing three months back. Human bones were found last week at a different dump site. The ID was made through dental records that the mother supplied after reporting her daughter missing. The young lady, who was a grocery store cashier named Casey Witherspoon, had a false tooth in the top front, so matching that up was easy."

"That means the cops found a skull?"

"Yep, and as gruesome as that sounds, it does help to have that irrefutable evidence."

"Well, that's gotta be good and bad news for her family."

I nodded. "Some families take that kind of news differently than others. The poor girl's parents nearly passed out from grief, but other times, family members are very stoic."

"Maybe they're just numb," Bob said.

Renz actually agreed with him for the first time since he'd met Bob. "Many families of crime victims are either frozen with grief or in shock. Their blank expression is often mistaken for indifference, but usually, that's the farthest thing from the truth."

"Yet a sad situation all around," Bob said.

Renz got back to business. "Did you bring along that list of names?"

"I did, and for clarification's sake, they aren't friends of mine." He chuckled. "They're just people I know of through the grapevine, and as far as the deeds they've committed, well, that's watercooler gossip. Either way, the men I've written down are the kind you don't want to be on the wrong side of, if you know what I mean. Half of them own swampland that's gone back generations, and the No Trespassing signs posted every hundred feet are meant to warn outsiders that if you step foot on their property uninvited, you may never walk out alive."

I let out a nervous laugh. "They really aren't that dangerous, are they?" Bob gave me a somber stare, and I quickly realized he was serious. "Then how the hell are we ever supposed to talk to those people?"

"You ever see that banjo movie?"

"*Deliverance*?"

"Yep, that's the one. Go ahead and multiply that tenfold."

"I don't understand why."

"And you don't have to. You aren't from these parts, and some people aren't the welcoming type. It's as simple as that."

I was baffled and slapped my hands against the table. "So now what?"

Bob shrugged. "I guess you could see if any have criminal records first and then decide if you want to go to their properties, but if you do, I'd have some deputies go along."

I sighed in despair. "We're never going to solve this damn crime."

"There's still the bones."

I turned to Bob. "What do you mean?"

"I have to see the actual bones so I can tell you if you're looking for a hunter or a butcher. The one-dimensional pictures didn't tell me what I needed to know. Seeing and touching the real bones will help narrow down your search. Or—"

"Or what?" Renz asked.

"Or find the worst of the worst offenders who live in the bayous and make up a reason to coax them into town. Getting them out of their own element is the safest and probably the only way to talk to them."

Renz stood and paced the room. He jangled the keys in his pocket and stared at the floor. "That isn't a half-bad idea, but how would we go about getting their attention?"

Robby's plan was working to perfection. He already had Jade convinced of his value, and it seemed like Agent DeLeon was slowly getting on board. They had nothing to work with on their own, but with Robby's help, they would likely solve the crime. He was sure they were thinking that very thing. "There's a little bar, actually a shed that was converted to a bar, on the far south end of Mechanicville on Llano Drive off Roland Road. It's called Trap House. That's where the sketchy locals hang out and could be the easiest way to talk to them outside their own turf."

Renz's forehead wrinkled. "Doesn't sound too inviting. Just more sketchy people in one place."

"Well, that's true. Then I'd suggest digging into their criminal history while Agent Monroe and I go to the forensic office and take a look at those bones."

"Yeah, I don't think—"

I interrupted Renz before he finished his sentence since I didn't need his protection. "It's fine, Renz, and we'll get more accomplished if we do several things at once."

He frowned. "Are you sure?"

"I'm positive, and we won't be gone long."

"Okay, if that's the way you want to do it. Got your phone?"

I grinned. "Yep, it's right in my purse." I reached out to Renz with my open hand. He reluctantly gave me the Explorer keys, and then I cocked my head toward the door. "Come on, Bob. It's my turn to drive."

Chapter 32

It was twelve forty by the time Bob and I arrived at the forensic and medical examiner's offices. We were lucky that everyone wasn't out on lunch breaks. When we entered the building and asked for the medical examiner or a member of the forensic team, the receptionist directed us to the cafeteria.

We thanked her and followed the hallway until it ended at the cafeteria, where the medical examiner, Louis Morrow, and one member of the forensic duo I'd met the other day, Hal Petrie, were enjoying their bag lunches at a table at the far end of the room. I hadn't had the privilege of meeting the medical examiner yet, so Hal made the introductions, and I introduced both of them to Bob.

Louis invited us to join them while they finished their food. Bob offered to grab two coffees from the vending machine while I explained to the men why we were there. When Bob took his seat, he added to the conversation by saying the knives used by a butcher had a different cut pattern than a knife used by a hunter.

"Makes sense," Hal said, "although I never compared

the types of knives used between them."

"I'd like to see the bones for myself. I'm a longtime hunter and know what kind of knives people in our trade use. Did the nicks and scrapes look the same on the bones from all the dump sites?"

Hal fielded that question since it was more of his expertise to make those kinds of comparisons. "Yes, under a microscope they did, but they were relatively faint."

"Is there a chance I could look at the bones? I'm working with Agent Monroe as a consultant."

I gave Hal a head tip. "I'll vouch for him. I want his expertise as a hunter, and hopefully, if he can identify the type of knife used, we can eliminate either a hunter or a butcher as our likely suspect."

"Sure, we can do that. The older bones are in cold storage, though, so that's Louis's department in the morgue area."

Louis wiped his mouth and tossed his paper napkin into the trash. "I'll get them ready for you while you work with Hal on the bones found on Monday."

Bob turned to me. "I'm ready whenever you are."

We followed Hal into the forensic lab, where we had to slip on gloves and lab coats to prevent us from contaminating anything.

"I have the bones that were discovered on Monday, right over here by the microscope. We've already determined by the two skulls found at the site that we have two different sets of remains and not any more. We've also determined that they're both female by the length of the femurs. We've compared them to the bones found at the first dump site, which we've determined to be from a male since the femur was a good four inches longer."

"And so far, only the bones from dump site two have been identified?"

"That's correct, Agent Monroe."

Bob spoke up. "Can you tell by the remains how any of the victims were killed?"

"Unfortunately not, Mr. Hebert."

Bob nodded.

"Okay, since the hip bone is relatively smooth and flat, the knife marks, or scrapes, I should say, are more noticeable on that particular bone. I have the hip bone from Jane Doe number one under there now. Go ahead and take a look."

I pointed with my chin, and Bob cozied up to the microscope.

"Yep, I can see the scrapes, and there are a few hard cuts that look like they came from a cleaver."

"And butchers use cleavers to separate large bones, don't they?" I asked.

"They do," Bob said. "The killer probably separated the hips from the legs and the spine with a cleaver. May I see the other hip bone found?"

"Sure thing." Hal moved the first one aside and placed the second one under the microscope. "This is Jane Doe number two."

Bob took a look. "The hard cuts aren't quite in the same spot, but it looks like the same utensil was used."

"Can I take a look?"

Bob moved away so I could check out the cuts myself. "So the only reason one would have to split apart a human body like this would be?" I noticed that Hal gave Bob a quick look but kept quiet. I turned to Bob and waited for an answer.

"Smaller body parts are easier to handle. As a hunter, we would do the same thing—separate the major limbs and then work on them individually by cutting away all the meat from the bones, like in this case, or separating the sections into cuts of meat, similar to T-bone steaks or any other cuts that include the bone."

I couldn't believe we were talking that casually about cutting apart a human body, but we were. I frowned at Bob. "So what are you saying? Who is the killer, a butcher or a hunter? You just said as a hunter, you would separate the limbs from the rest of the body so handling the sections would be easier for you to cut the meat off the bone."

"To be honest, Jade, even though a cleaver was used, I'm leaning more toward the killer being a hunter. He's going to want all the meat off the bones before disposing of them. A butcher just might turn everything into a cut of meat as if he was working on a steer. It wouldn't be unreasonable for a hunter to have a cleaver, and I didn't see marks that reminded me of a boning knife."

"What's a boning knife?"

"A thin sharp knife that curves up to a sharp point. Every butcher uses them." He pointed at the hip bone still under the microscope. "What we saw there looked like amateur cuts to me, not like they were done on a large table in a butcher shop."

"So you're definitely leaning toward the killer being a hunter, just like Mark and Billy said?"

Bob rubbed his chin before answering. "Well, I guess I am."

"Okay, let's take a look at those older bones just to see if we notice the same type of cuts. If we do, I'd be confident enough to say all of the bones that have been found were dumped by the same perpetrator."

Chapter 33

It was after two o'clock by the time we got back to the sheriff's office. Deputy Polsen said they'd cleared all the butchers who had questionable backgrounds, and that made me believe Bob's theory of the killer being a hunter even more.

As we entered our makeshift office, I saw Renz tapping away on the computer. He looked up and stopped what he was doing. I plopped down in the chair next to him, and Bob remained standing until I pointed at the chair across from me. "Take a load off."

"Okay, thanks."

Renz leaned back, stretched, and asked if we had discovered anything.

"Bob thinks the killer is a hunter."

Renz squeezed the bridge of his nose. "Damn. A butcher would be a lot easier to deal with. The reasoning is?"

"Lack of precise cuts or attention to detail. Kind of amateurish in my opinion," Bob said. "I'd imagine since a butcher has to make meat look presentable, it would just cross over into any meat he was cutting. I may be wrong, but I'm just stating what I observed."

Renz nodded. "Yeah, and that coincides with what Mark and Billy said. Maybe the three of you should discuss it together with us. Everyone give their opinion, a brainstorming session of sorts. They might even think of more names to throw in the hat."

"Maybe," Bob said.

I jotted that down on my rapidly growing to-do list. "I'll arrange it. Did you come up with anything as far as the names Bob gave you?"

Renz let out a puff of air. "A few, but they're misdemeanor offenses and nothing that should progress into murder and dismemberment. I think it would be easier for a handful of us to stop in on those fellas and have a talk with them."

Bob chuckled. "Mind if I sit that one out? I wouldn't want them to think I'm some kind of snitch. Next thing you know, I'd be on the dinner menu."

I wrinkled my face. "That's disgusting."

Bob huffed. "You're right, but it could also be true."

Renz picked three men who'd had multiple run-ins with the law, and they came to the forefront only because they were often seen around town raising hell.

"I'll see if Conway will give us a couple of deputies to help out, just in case any of those three try to take matters into their own hands."

"One question," Bob said.

Renz turned to him. "Yeah, what's that?"

"How are you going to determine if any of them are the killer?"

"We'll look around their property, talk to acquaintances, and see if they have solid alibis for the last few days. Essentially, it's the same kind of measures we use for any murder case."

Bob stood. "Then I guess I'll head out if you don't need me for anything else today."

"Thanks, Bob," I said. "You've been a big help."

He nodded, wished us luck, and left.

Chapter 34

Robby arrived home at five o'clock. With the money he'd taken out of Mark and Billy's wallets, he had enough to stop at an auto supply store in Houma and buy a paint sprayer, a gallon of black auto paint, and plenty of tape. That red pickup would be tough to cover with a light-colored paint, so black it would be. Black was a safe color, didn't stand out, and wouldn't attract unnecessary attention. He'd get to it in his spare time but wouldn't be able to take the truck out on the road until the agents left Louisiana. Jade knew what he drove, and it sure as hell wasn't a newer-model red or black Dodge Ram.

I should park that truck in the garage for the time being. I'll be painting it in there, anyway, and if by a stroke of bad luck Billy did tell his wife where he was going, that truck would be a dead giveaway that I did something to him if it was seen on my property.

Inside the shack, Robby found the keys right where he'd left them—in a coffee cup in the kitchen cupboard. After pulling the tarp off the truck and clearing space for it in the garage, Robby drove it in, locked the truck doors, and returned the keys to the house. It was time to check on his guests. He doused himself from head to toe with bug spray—late afternoon was when mosquitos were the worst—then grabbed Mark's rifle and the ammo he'd brought with him that morning and headed out. The wild boars usually became active around five o'clock. No matter what, he wasn't about to take any chances, especially since he didn't use Pete as a hunting dog. One hound working alone would be an easy target for a hungry pig.

Keeping his head on a swivel, Robby walked deeper and deeper into the swampy mosquito-ridden wetlands. Within minutes, he would arrive at the trees the men were tied to. Even though darkness wouldn't take over the sky for a few hours, the sun had dropped, the tree cover was thick, and a flashlight was in his pocket if he needed it. He kept his distance from the water, knowing full well that alligators rested along the banks in the evening and waited for animals to come down to the water's edge to drink.

Robby heard moaning in the distance. He was almost there and had his gun at the ready since he wasn't sure what he would find and didn't want to go in unprepared. That could prove to be the biggest mistake he ever made—if he lived to tell the story.

He flicked on the flashlight to look for any eyes glowing nearby. There weren't any, but there were definite signs of damage to Billy.

"Holy shit. Take a look at you, Billy." Robby moved in cautiously and shined the light in the man's face. It was covered in bug bites with swollen red welts. He pointed the light at Billy's leg, which had been eaten from the knee down. The pigs must have smelled the blood and taken advantage of the opportunity. It was a horrific sight, and the man was barely alive.

Using his flashlight, Robby scanned the area again to make sure there wasn't a pig coming back for seconds, or thirds, then he tapped Billy's face with the rifle's barrel and saw some slight movement.

"You don't have long for this world, man. Maybe I'll come back in the morning, cut you down, and let the pigs feast on what's left of your sorry ass." He turned to Mark, who was still somewhat alert. Mark's eyes bulged as Robby came closer. "How's it going, Mark? Enjoying the boar hunt?" Robby laughed and poked Mark's shoulder with his own gun. The man moaned, clearly in agony. "Man up. It can't be that bad. At least you don't have pigs or gators gnawing on your body yet." He pointed his thumb over his shoulder at Billy and shook his head. "You gotta wonder how that feels, right? Maybe I'll let you find out, but first, I want to check your restraints. I bet about now you wish you did have a wife. Somebody who'd give a crap that you went missing. I'm sure nobody even knows, and hell, Billy and his old lady got into a fight before he left home this morning. That's the best-case scenario I can think of. I bet she won't even report him missing for a day or two. She probably thinks he left to cool off or teach her a lesson. Nobody is going to ask me a damn thing about either of you since I've been working with the FBI and have daily alibis. I'd never be a suspect. You went missing and were never found, end of story." He leaned in close to Mark's mosquito-bitten face and slapped his hands together. "Poof! You both disappeared without a trace, and to be honest, I doubt if anyone cares."

Robby did a slow circle around the tree that Mark was tied to and tugged on the ropes. They were still tight, and the tape over them was secure. Billy didn't matter. Soon enough, he would be pig food.

"Looks like you're good to go. So did you get a chance to watch the pigs eat Billy's leg?"

Mark's eyes darted left and right as he focused on every move Robby made. He tried to speak, but the tape over his mouth made his words sound like gibberish.

"I can't understand you." Robby smashed a mosquito that had landed on Mark's forehead. "See what a great guy I am. I killed that sucker." He cupped his hand to his ear and moved in close to Mark's mouth. "What? You said thank you? Sure, pal, not a problem. I bet you're wondering why I picked you and Billy to be pig food, right? It's simple, really. You guys happened on my dumping ground when you were out hunting. You did the right thing and called the *pigs*."

Robby let out a roaring laugh, bent over, and slapped his knees. "I can't believe how clever I am with words. Damn it all!" He wiped his eyes and continued. "Anyway, sure as shit, if I don't drive down Bayou Dularge Road and see a deputy's car blocking that old driveway. Well, I knew it was just my luck that two assholes decided to go back there and hunt before the pigs had a chance to finish off the remains.

Then I had to insert myself in the investigation, you know, to stay one step ahead of the FBI. Your names came up, I told them I knew you boys as hunters, and then I decided to exact karma on you. Now you're the prey, and the pigs are the hunters. I'll give up two kills of my own and let the pigs have you. It's the least I can do. My cooler has enough meat in it to last a few weeks, anyway. After the FBI leaves, I'll get busy again, but for now, those idiots are paying me to help them." He roared with laughter again. "You just can't make that shit up." Robby paced around the fifty-foot area and looked back and forth between the men.

"Yep, that'll work." He returned to Mark's side. "Are you ready? Here's the plan."

Chapter 35

We'd spent the last hour discussing how the interviews would go, and we still weren't done. Renz had checked and double-checked what the law had on those three men, and although what he'd found wasn't substantial, talking to each one could provide us with information on people who actually were dangerous.

I studied the map of the parish, which Renz had pulled up earlier. He'd located each address, and we would start with the home of Leroy Duggar, the man who lived closest to town and had the most frequent flyer points at the local jail. He'd been arrested for starting bar fights. He lived at the end of Dickson Road, only a hop, skip, and a jump from his favorite haunt—Trap House. According to the records, Leroy had an eighty-acre parcel that butted up to a large canal that went in every direction. If necessary, and if he had a boat, Leroy could make a quick exit on the water and easily lose someone who didn't know the area well.

According to his most recent arrest, which was only a month earlier, Leroy had been bailed out of jail by his twenty-nine-year-old son, Zeke, whose address was shown to be the same as Leroy's.

"So this Zeke may be at the residence too." Renz looked from one deputy to the other. "Either of you ever had a run-in with the son?"

They both said they hadn't.

"Well, that's good. Hopefully, he's the level-headed one out of the two. After that, we'll call on Teddy Cain. He's been arrested three times for battery. Apparently, he enjoys beating up his wife."

I tapped my notes with my pen. "So that means he could have a volatile temper and be more dangerous than a drunk who likes to break barstools over people's heads."

Cassidy nodded. "True, but we've dealt with him before. We know how to handle him."

"Good to know," Renz said.

"And the third guy was who?" I asked.

"Derrick Alamane. He lives almost to Dulac and is definitely a bayou man through and through. He won't come quietly if he's arrested. His record shows that he's resisted arrest more than a dozen times."

I frowned. "And he's never spent any length of time in jail?"

Deputy Stillman spoke up. "Nope. Every offense was for petty theft. He just didn't enjoy the part where he got arrested. It usually took three deputies to get him into the back seat of the squad car."

"This sounds like a job better suited for the locals," I said.

"That may be true, Jade, but since we aren't hitting

home runs with anything else, and because of the chance that someone may have something worthwhile to say, we're going to conduct each interview ourselves. The deputies are coming along for insurance in case something goes sideways." Renz stood and gathered his notes. He passed everything to me, and I placed it inside my briefcase.

"We should all vest up," Stillman said. "Bayou folks, whether they have records or not, are still unpredictable. They don't like authority figures, especially when they're trespassing on their land."

We took off with only a few hours of daylight left. If we were lucky enough to find someone willing to chat, we might not finish the interviews until the next day. Otherwise, we were back to square one—no witnesses to a crime and no leads to follow up on.

We headed out in two vehicles—Renz and I in ours, and deputies Stillman and Cassidy in the squad car leading the way. First, we would hit Leroy Duggar's property, which was southwest of Mechanicville along the expansive canals.

It took less than fifteen minutes to get there. Stillman pulled off to the shoulder of the road, and Renz snugged in behind him and rolled down the window.

"What's up?"

"I think we should lead the way in. They'll see it's law enforcement and might not be as agitated as they would be if an unmarked and unidentified vehicle just drove in like they had an invitation."

"Okay, that makes sense. You feel safe?"

Stillman shrugged. "Never did business with the man on

his own turf. We'll try to keep our intrusion as low-key as possible and see if he cooperates."

When Renz rolled up the window, I shook my head. "Good God, it's like we're going in after a Colombian drug cartel instead of a US citizen who just wants to be left alone."

"That may be true, but the likelihood of every person we talk to today having a gun in hand, or one close by, is probably high."

I kept my eyes peeled for movement of any kind as we followed the deputies down the narrow lane that was only wide enough for one vehicle coming in or going out. I snapped my fingers. "We could be surrounded just like that with nowhere to go."

Renz looked my way and rolled his eyes. "Don't go all weird on me. Stay in the moment and watch your surroundings."

I kept quiet, but if Renz had the slightest idea of the dangerous shit I'd been through in my law enforcement career, he probably wouldn't consider my concerns "going weird" on him. I was already on my second round of nine lives, and I wasn't inviting trouble, just reliving my past.

The lane—or driveway, I assumed—was at least a half mile long with dense forests of old-growth oak and cypress trees around us. "Why the hell are all the driveways so long?"

"Because the houses are on or near the water. People fish, boat, and hunt by the waterways. It's their life blood. Why build a house next to the road and then walk all the way to the water? That wouldn't make sense."

"Yeah, I guess you're right." I pointed. "Hey, I think I see a rooftop in the distance."

"Yep, I see it too. Time to watch closely for a person, a dog, or something else."

"You got it, partner."

The squad car's brake lights flashed. Stillman had almost reached the clearing where multiple buildings were located. The lane ended and opened to a wide area where a stilt house sat back by the water, and several outbuildings were closer to us. So far, we hadn't seen a thing, not even a mangy dog. Stillman continued on and turned in front of the outbuildings until his car was pointed back at the lane. We did the same, but now ours was the vehicle closest to the buildings. I didn't know if we were being watched, but I absolutely felt exposed.

"Should we get out?"

Renz stared at the squad car ahead of us. "They're wearing the uniforms and have a marked car. There." He pointed. "It looks like Stillman is going to make the first move."

We watched out our windshield, and as soon as Stillman opened his door and exposed his left leg, a shot rang out and sprayed up dirt about five feet to the side of the squad car. Stillman quickly slammed the door.

I spun in my seat. "What the hell!"

A voice from behind us shouted out. "What do you want, and why are you here? You're on private property, and I have signs posted everywhere."

I shook my head. "The guy is right. None of us were

invited here, and he means business. So now what?"

Renz pointed. "Hang on. It looks like Stillman is lowering his window."

The deputy yelled back to our vehicle. "What do you agents want to do?"

"Let me do the talking," Renz said.

I snapped my head toward my partner. "You aren't getting out, are you?"

Renz gave me a concerned look. "We both are. You did put on that vest, right?"

"Of course I did, but it doesn't protect my head."

"Okay, just don't do anything until I tell you to." Renz opened his car door slowly and yelled out his name and title and said he wanted to speak with Leroy Duggar.

The same male voice responded, and as hard as I tried, I couldn't put eyes on him. I had no idea where he was watching us from, but he sounded like he was in or near the stilt house.

"What do you want with my pa, and why are those deputies with you?"

"So that's Zeke talking," I said.

Renz nodded and continued. "They're here to assist in case you do what you're doing—threatening our lives. All we want to do is speak with your father, or you if he isn't home. We have no beef with either of you. We just want to ask some questions."

"Get out of the car and go tell those deputies to leave. After they're gone, you can come up to the house. Pull anything and I'll shoot you dead and cite the stand-my-ground rights."

"Shit, Renz, why don't we have any binos in this damn vehicle, and what are you going to do?"

He shrugged. "We need information, don't we?"

"Yeah, but I doubt if he or his 'pa' are going to admit that they murdered and chopped up people."

Beads of sweat had popped up on Renz's forehead. I handed him a damp wipe.

"Thanks." He ran the cloth across his face then balled it up and tossed it in the footwell. "I guess I'm going to do what he said, but I'll tell Stillman to wait at the end of the driveway. If they hear gunshots, they better get their asses back here and fast."

I cursed. We would be on our own with no idea of the Duggar men's mindset.

"Just keep looking back at the house while I go talk to Stillman and Cassidy."

"I got your six, partner." I knew—and I was sure Renz did too—that my handgun would be useless at that distance and against somebody I couldn't even see. No matter what, I prayed for his safety and watched for movement near the house.

It took only a minute before Renz was back at the car. He climbed into the driver's seat, let out what sounded like a relieved sigh, then watched out the windshield as Stillman drove away and out of sight.

"So?"

Renz lowered his window again. "I guess we wait for instructions."

As soon as the dust settled from the squad car leaving,

Zeke yelled out to us. "Who's with you?"

Renz cupped his hand against his mouth and yelled back. "My partner, Agent Jade Monroe, is with me. We came to Louisiana together at the request of the Houma Sheriff's Office."

"Relating to what?"

"Has the sheriff's office gone public with the story?" I asked before Renz responded.

Renz shrugged. "I don't know about papers or TV. All I know is word of mouth spreads quickly, and I'm sure Billy Bennett and Mark LaFleur told everyone they know about the bones they found."

"Shit. We'd be showing our hand if we tell them why we've come and they actually *are* the perps. It's a dangerous thing to do, Renz."

Renz yelled out the window. "There's been a rash of Terrebonne Parish folks that have gone missing lately. We were told that you might be able to give us some names that local law enforcement isn't familiar with who could be engaged in illegal activities."

"What are you insinuating?"

The voice asking had changed. I looked at Renz. "That has to be Leroy."

"I'm not insinuating anything, sir. We just want to help the community and get opinions from people who know and hear news that the sheriff's office doesn't have access to."

We waited.

"You aren't here to bust my chops for anything?"

"No, sir. We just want to talk."

"All right. The woman gets out first, and she needs to place her sidearm on the ground. After that, you get out and do the same. When I see both of your weapons lying in the dirt, I'll meet you in front of the house."

"Son of a bitch."

"Jade, if we stay calm and don't come off as confrontational, we should be fine. Remember, he only has a misdemeanor record for bar fights."

Chapter 36

Apprehensively, I climbed out of the Explorer and faced the stilt house, which I was sure I was being watched from. I slowly lifted my Glock from the holster and placed it on the ground.

"Now, walk forward ten feet."

I did as instructed.

Renz was told to do the same thing—and did. We were standing ten feet away from our weapons and facing someone we couldn't put eyes on.

"Come toward my voice and then sit on those stumps by the firepit."

We walked another fifty feet and sat on stumps that I assumed were meant to be used as seats around the evening fires. A minute later, two men appeared from the back of the house where the door likely was. They took seats across from us and sized us up in seconds.

"Feds, huh?"

Renz nodded. "That's correct. I assume you're Leroy?" He looked at the elder of the two then turned to the younger one. "And Zeke?"

"Yep, now let's hear what you want so you aren't wasting our night. I was about to make supper."

My mind went to a dark place when Leroy said that, but I needed to stay focused on the moment. Because this was good ol' boy country, Renz would do the talking. I was just there as a backup agent without a gun.

"Like I said, we're looking into the claims of people who've gone missing from the parish—more than what is reasonable in that short amount of time."

"Why'd you decide to come here? We haven't abducted anyone."

"To be honest, it's because we're outsiders without any knowledge of what local folks hear—the kind of talk that law enforcement isn't privy to."

Zeke laughed. "So because you aren't local law enforcement, we should just blurt out everything we know to you instead? I don't know where you're from, but down here in Louisiana, we have a thing called loyalty to our own."

Renz stared at the charred wood in the firepit. "And we understand that, but we also understand the worries of each family that has missing loved ones. We've been here for several days and don't have a single lead as far as people who are edgy, questionable, or downright involved in illegal activities. All we need are names of other folks we can talk to. Following up on those names could lead us to the perpetrators." Renz looked from one face to the other. "We'd really appreciate your help."

Leroy stoked the fire then jerked his head at me. "What

do you have to say, little lady?"

Normally, a comment like that would have set me off, but I knew better than to start anything.

"Mr. Duggar, we've spoken with some of the families whose loved ones have gone missing, and not knowing the whereabouts of their own children, sisters, or brothers is killing them. Some of the missing people are kids still in high school. It's obvious that you love your son and care about his well-being. We just want to help those families find out if their loved ones are alive or dead."

Leroy drew designs in the ashes while I talked. I hoped I was making an impression on him and his son.

"Uh-huh. Okay, so you're looking for names of people with questionable intentions? Recluses, I imagine, that the law shies away from or doesn't know exist?"

"That's exactly the people we need to speak with, or folks who are into voodoo and the occult. Just like the sheriff's office, we don't know who those people are."

Leroy squinted, looked from Renz to me, and laughed. "You two have big balls, and I like that. You waltz in here without guns and talk civilly to us."

My thoughts, which I kept to myself, were that we didn't have much choice.

"Bravery is a quality that I admire, so yeah, we'll give you a few names, but nobody better find out who they came from."

Renz nodded. "And you have our word on that."

Leroy and Zeke said they knew of two local men and two who lived a distance out. We would focus on the ones who lived closer to Houma first then check out the other two if need be.

Leroy began. "I don't know anyone who engages in the occult, or black magic, some would say, and voodoo is more about sacrificial spiritualism. I can't help you with any of those practices or people who engage in them, so we'll start with John Cavanaugh. He's a pisser of a man if I ever saw one."

I didn't know the definition of a pisser, but I assumed it was bad.

Zeke stood. "Before we continue, I'm going to grab a few beers." He looked at Renz and me, almost daring us to refuse his hospitality. We both thanked him and said we'd appreciate a beer. I took it as a peace offering.

Minutes later and with a refreshing brew in front of me, I listened as Leroy continued with the names. I pulled my notepad and pen from my pants pocket and was ready to write.

"Before I go on, I just want you to know that my boy and me aren't bad people. Sure, I drink too much and get arrested for it, but I don't take part in criminal activity, and that's the difference between us and some other folks."

"Understood." Renz tipped his head for Leroy to continue.

Leroy, a gray-haired man who looked like he hadn't run a comb through his hair in a month and who lisped through the spaces of missing teeth, went on about John Cavanaugh.

"John beats everything and everyone in sight. He's mean, mad, and malicious. The wife and kids are usually black and blue, and his animals die more often than any animal should."

Zeke added his take. "He beats his critters and then shoots them. He'd probably do the same to his family if the law wouldn't find out and throw his ass in prison. He makes moonshine, drinks way too much of it, and sells the rest. He forces his daughters to entertain men for money."

I winced at the story Zeke was telling us and couldn't believe the law wasn't aware of John's actions.

"He lives just outside Crozier along Bayou Dularge Road."

I wrote that down then gave Renz a quick glance. Crozier was within a few miles of the last dump site, and John sounded like someone who could be a suspect.

After a gulp of beer, Leroy added Evan Millbrook to the list. "There's something mentally wrong with that man. I don't think he does what he does out of spite. I just think he's crazy. He kills wild game, skins it, and eats the organs raw. Says something about the organ meat giving him power and clarity. Those stories come from bar talk when everyone is three sheets to the wind—including myself—but I know them to be true."

I felt my face contort and knew Evan could be a suspect, too, even if he was deemed mentally unfit. Zeke said Evan lived on the outskirts of Houma in Mandalay.

"Who else can you think of?"

"There's Robby Williams from Dulac, about a half hour south of Houma. He owns a lot of land and lives in a stilt house like mine. The man doesn't work, yet I see him in local bars on occasion. He definitely likes the ladies."

"And why would you include him?" Renz asked.

Leroy swatted at a pesky mosquito. "Can't put my finger on it, really. He's just sketchy as hell and an opportunist. He'll steal your car out from under your nose if he has an extra second, and has done it a number of times. I've seen him steal purses off the barstool backs when ladies go to the restroom, and he'll steal tip money right off the bar and pocket it. Best to look the other way, because if you confront him, he'll beat your ass."

I wrote the name down. "Okay, and what about the last guy?"

Zeke took that question. "Who do you think, Pa? Destin Orly?"

"Yep, Destin for sure. He lives outside McBride, north of here. He's bragged about the number of times he's held guns to people's heads."

I frowned. "But why? What's his reason?"

"He owns an auto repair shop, and if you don't pay your bill in cash on the day the repair work is done, he pulls out that Smith & Wesson .45 he keeps behind the counter and sticks the business end of it against your temple then empties your wallet himself. I've heard plenty of stories about him and keep my distance from him and his shop. He has a hair-trigger temper, and that's not what you want when a gun is pressed into your face."

I let out a long breath. "You guys have certainly been helpful. We don't know if any of these men are who we're looking for, but the more people we talk to the better. We'll narrow it down in the next few days. I'm sure of it." After we took our final gulps of beer, Renz and I thanked them for their help and returned to the Explorer, where we picked up our guns and left.

"Well, that was a first for me." I groaned in relief.

Renz laughed. "I've been in the FBI for years, and it's a first for me too."

I shook my head as I thought about the names that Leroy and Zeke had given us. "If our greeting from those two was a warning shot, what do we have in store for us from the real scary people?"

"Don't know, but we'll find out tomorrow. There's no way in hell I'm stepping foot on anyone's property at night. Let's head back in and see what we can find on the two guys who live closest to town."

Chapter 37

It was nearly dark by the time we took our seats in our office space. We each had a drive-through restaurant hamburger and fries in front of us, and I was famished.

Renz called Conway in to update him, and it sounded like he'd already heard Stillman's account of what took place before they headed down the Duggar driveway.

After popping a fry into my mouth, I shook my head. "Yeah, that was unexpected and definitely started our visit off on the wrong foot. Thank God it didn't get any more serious than that."

Conway held up his hand. "I just want to be clear on a few things so you don't have the wrong idea of southern Louisiana folks."

We gave him our full attention.

"Sure, go ahead," I said.

"We have our fair share of bad apples in the bushel basket, no different than in any other state. Look at all the crime and murders that go on daily in Chicago. It's every weekend, for Pete's sake."

I knew that far too well. At Jesse's wedding reception,

he'd mentioned how the murders in Chicago had increased dramatically over the last year, but anyone who watched the news would know that.

"Louisiana is a great state to live in, and the people are mostly friendly, law-abiding folks. They're good people. We have outcasts here, recluses, and just downright crazy people, but they're the exception, not the rule."

"We understand that completely and couldn't agree more. We've met some very nice individuals, and we definitely aren't biased. Our job takes us to areas where we're actively searching for the worst of the worst. It's what we do, and we hold no animosity toward anyone. All we want is to find the killer and bring him to justice, nothing else."

Conway nodded. "Good. I didn't want you to think our state was filled with bad characters."

Renz said his peace. "And we don't. Actually, after the dust settled earlier"—he looked at me and grinned—"it turned out that Leroy and Zeke Duggar were decent, helpful people."

I chuckled. "Zeke even offered us a beer. Who would have thought?"

Renz continued. "Anyway, we got four names from them, and two of those four live in the area. We'll talk to them tomorrow. I wasn't about to trespass on a stranger's property at night."

"Smart thinking," Conway said.

I added my opinion. "I still think it might be helpful to sit Bob, Mark, and Billy down together. Maybe they've come across another hunter in the woods who seemed a bit off. Anything they could give us would help. We need a lead and damn soon since we can't stay here forever if we have nothing to work with. Leroy didn't know anyone who is into the occult, so that angle will have to sit on the back burner unless your deputies can ask around."

"I'll task some of them with doing that tomorrow."

Renz took over. "Do you know John Cavanaugh or Evan Millbrook?"

Conway rubbed his chin. "Can't say that I do. People come and go, especially when property remains in the same family for generations and gets passed down to out of the area nephews, cousins, and the like. If they're bad folks and we don't know of them, then they're deliberately staying under the radar."

"Sounds that way. We'll call on them first and then check into the others who live a distance out of town. There's still more people to talk to that your deputies said they've also had run-ins with. Tomorrow is going to be a full day of interviews."

"And my guys can pitch in anywhere you need them."

"Appreciate it," Renz said before he took the last bite of his cheeseburger and licked his fingers. He looked at me and shook his head. "I should have ordered two."

We spent the next hour checking into whatever we could find on John Cavanaugh and Evan Millbrook, which was little to nothing. We located the property tax records that had been changed through the years to reflect new owners as people died and passed on the land to their next of kin.

Little else showed up for either of them—no job records, no income tax statements, no utility bills.

I leaned back, cracked my neck left to right, and let out a discouraged sigh. "Renz, what if this case goes unsolved? There's at least three dump sites that have been discovered over the last month. Who knows if there's more out—"

"I guarantee you there's more. Why would the killer stop doing what he's doing, especially if he likes what he does and knows there's little chance of getting caught? We literally have nothing to work with, not even a sighting of anyone suspicious out in the woods."

"Of course we don't. I mean, who the hell goes out to those remote locations on purpose except hunters?"

Renz corrected me. "And killers."

"Yeah, and that. If the killer is anything like the guys who live off the grid and doesn't even have a driver's license on record, he'll remain a ghost forever."

"Yep, and we'll move on to a new case in a new city. Just because we're in the Serial Crimes Unit doesn't mean we solve every case, Jade."

"I know, I know."

Renz stood. "Come on. Let's get the hell out of here and go have a drink in the hotel lounge. I might even order an appetizer too."

I grinned. "You don't have to ask me twice."

Chapter 38

Robby had just finished eating supper and had fed Pete and the cats. With full bellies, the animals seemed content. Pete lay on the weather-decayed wooden deck while the cats wandered off to do what feral cats did at night.

"Better watch your asses out there," Robby yelled. "Doubt if the hogs are still hungry, but I bet there are plenty of gators who would consider you felines a nice evening snack."

Robby went to the cooler, cracked open a can of beer, and returned to the firepit. He took his seat and wondered how the activity had played out back in the woods. He would have loved to watch firsthand, but the likelihood of personal injury was too great to take a chance. He would have probably been the third course in the pigs' nightly feast.

I'll walk back there in the morning and see if either of them are still alive before I head into Houma.

As Robby reminisced on that morning's trip into the woods, he remembered Billy's condition. There wasn't a chance in hell he would live through the night. Before leaving the woods, Robby had cut Billy down and decided to let nature, or the pigs, take its course. He was pretty sure that by morning, there wouldn't be a trace of Billy left.

Maybe clothes. Don't know if pigs are stupid enough to eat clothing or not. Guess we'll see.

He laughed when he thought about what he'd whispered to Mark. He remembered how Mark's eyes had bulged. "They nearly popped out of their sockets."

Robby had stepped back twenty yards and fired two rounds—one into each of Mark's legs. That way, the pigs could reach the fresh wounds and tear the meat from Mark's bones.

"Nah, I bet they just eat the bones too. Man, what I'd give to be a bird in a tree and watch all of that unfold right in front of me. I bet there are sickos who would pay hundreds of dollars to watch that in real time. I'd offer that to the public if people could keep their mouths shut, but I know that would never happen. I'd be a rich son of a bitch, though."

Robby heard in the distance the distinct sound of a gator growl and water splashing. Hissing and a cat screech followed that commotion, then everything went quiet.

"Damn cats never learn. Sounds like another one just became gator food."

Chapter 39

After two gin and tonics and a mixed appetizer tray, Renz and I parted ways at our hotel rooms. We agreed to meet in the breakfast room at seven o'clock the next morning. I couldn't wait to crawl into bed, but because we'd been sitting around Leroy's firepit, a smoky odor lingered in my hair and clothes. I needed a shower and headed to the bathroom before I got too comfortable.

By nine o'clock, I was sitting in bed, had gone through my daily emails, and had run my fingers through my hair. It was still damp. I figured after a half-hour phone call to Amber, my hair would be dry, and I would get the daily updates on life back home too.

I tapped her number, set the phone to Speaker, and leaned back against the headboard. The local news was muted in the background, and the weather report showed another hot and humid ninety-degree day waiting for us. My hair would be nothing but frizz, but at least it would be clean.

Amber answered as I'd expected—her cheerful self. I was fortunate to have a happy-go-lucky sister who was also a great cook. I looked forward to getting back home, eating her comfort food, and sleeping in my own bed.

"Hey, big sis, what's the word?"

I sighed. "I wish I could tell you we caught the killer and we're flying back home tomorrow, but—"

"But you haven't? Geez, what's the problem? I thought you were with the elite team now."

I chuckled. "Murderers don't care what our titles are. If they're smart, stealthy, and steadfast, it's tough to catch them, especially when nobody has seen any crimes being committed."

"Humph."

"And when the stories we've heard about some bayou people are actually true, it's hard."

"Meaning?"

"Meaning they don't like outsiders up in their business. There's sketchy people down here, Amber, and southern Louisiana is definitely a world apart from Milwaukee."

"So what are you going to do?"

"Keep plugging along. We have a good number of people to interview tomorrow as long as we live through it."

"You're joking, right? Tell me you're joking."

"I'm joking. You've got nothing to worry about. Everything is fine, and I have—"

"Yeah, I know, and you have a big gun, but I bet those swampers have big guns too."

I wasn't about to tell her of the incident with Leroy and Zeke earlier in the day. We were a family of cops, and Amber was well aware of the risks that involved, and I couldn't think of a good reason to make her worry any more than necessary.

She told me the latest on what was going on at the sheriff's office back home—nothing too far from the usual petty crimes, and usually, their day consisted of serving arrest warrants. At times, the small-town simplicity sounded nice. It kept everyone's blood pressure and heart rate in check. It could also become boring and repetitive, although we'd all had our share of psychotic criminals to deal with. I'd moved on to the FBI and then on to a more targeted branch of the FBI, chasing cases across the United States as needed.

Amber and I said our good nights, but before I hung up, I told her that I loved her and wanted meat loaf, mashed potatoes, and corn on the cob for supper on the first night I was back. She promised me we would have that, said she loved me, too, and hung up. I smiled, felt my hair—it was dry—and switched off the light.

The alarm on my phone blasted in my ear. "No way it's morning yet." It took maximum effort to crack open my eyes since it felt like they were glued closed. I squinted in the direction of the window, and daylight came through the slats of the blinds. "Damn it. How did eight hours go by so fast?"

With a groan, I tossed the blankets aside and climbed out of bed. I started the four-cup coffeemaker then did a quick rinse in the shower to wake up. I had planned to meet Renz downstairs in forty-five minutes for a big breakfast, since there was a good chance we would miss lunch, and then head to the sheriff's office.

After two cups of coffee, I got ready for the day, which included pulling my hair back in a ponytail. Long thick hair on a humid day was not something I needed to deal with, and getting it away from my face and off my neck was the way to go. With a final look in the mirror, I grabbed my gear and room key and headed downstairs.

Renz had already picked a table and had two cups of coffee poured when I arrived.

"How'd you sleep?" he asked.

"Wonderfully, but lounging in bed for another hour would have been even better."

"I know what you mean. I talked to Taft a few minutes ago and gave her our latest since Tuesday night when I spoke to her last."

I took a sip of coffee. "And?"

"And she asked if you were behaving."

I swatted his arm. "She did not!"

Renz laughed. "Nah, she actually asked if we needed help, as in a few more agents. I told her there was no point in that since we haven't gotten a reliable lead to follow up on yet. She's giving us two more days before she pulls us back to Milwaukee."

"Seriously?"

"I'm afraid so."

"Humph. Then what?"

"Then it's considered an unsolved case."

I pondered that for a moment and didn't like the idea of giving up on an ongoing investigation, but since I wasn't the one in charge, it wasn't up to me. "Okay, I guess. So, what's on the menu?"

"Same thing as yesterday and the day before. Not complaining, though. The breakfast here is pretty good," Renz said.

"I agree, so we should dig in. We've got a long day ahead of us, and who knows what kind of trouble we might get into with John Cavanaugh and Evan Millbrook."

"Yeah, that'd be funny if it wasn't a real possibility. I think we should team up with a couple of deputies and ride along in their squad car. Four armed cops are better than none."

I shook my head at the memories from yesterday. They were funny now but not so much then, and we needed to be careful.

I tipped my head toward the long counter of food and grabbed a plate. "Come on. I'm starving."

After four pancakes, hash browns, three strips of bacon, a banana, and a cup of yogurt, I was done. That meal would easily hold me over until suppertime. I finished my cup of coffee and was ready to go.

Renz jammed two more strips of bacon into his mouth. "Now I'm ready. We'll see if Conway can spare a few deputies, and then we'll hit the road. We have a lot of ground to cover today."

"What about Bob?"

"Damn, I forgot about him." Renz tipped his wrist and checked the time. "If he isn't at the station by nine o'clock, we're leaving. He didn't want to be part of going to people's homes, and after yesterday's fiasco at the Duggar house, we can't take a civilian along to a potentially dangerous situation, anyway."

"I agree, and if he stops in, we'll just have to say we don't need his help today."

Chapter 40

With his rifle slung over his shoulder, Robby walked parallel to the water but far enough away to stay safe. The woods where he'd left Mark and Billy were another ten-minute walk away, and he was curious to see what if anything had unfolded last night. He'd already worn a path into the ground cover from the half dozen times he'd gone back and forth. He sipped his coffee as he walked, but he would leave his cup along the trail once he got closer. Having his rifle ready to shoot was far more important, especially when closing in on the wild pigs' nesting ground and their likely food source.

Robby slowed to a stop, cocked his ear, and listened. He was fifty yards from where he'd tied the men to the trees, and he should be able to hear if a ruckus was going on in the woods. He set the coffee cup on a log and slowly inched ahead. Stopping every twenty feet, he listened for the grunts of wild boars. He waited at the edge of the woods and kept silent as he squinted into the thick brush and looked for movement. That was when he heard the rutting and grunts.

If I ease my way in and shoot to scare them away, I should be fine. I need to see what they've accomplished overnight.

Robby raised the rifle and fired off two shots. He heard the pigs scatter and moved in cautiously. His eyes needed a minute to adjust to the darkened woods, then he saw the carnage.

"Holy shit."

He moved in closer to what was left of Billy. Seeing bits and pieces of clothing and a few rib bones was the only way to know for sure that a human body had once been inside those shredded jeans and strips of plaid shirt. Robby found one mangled boot. The other probably went missing yesterday when the pigs made quick work of Billy's wounded leg. Robby continued on to the tree where only the upper half of Mark's body remained. He grimaced as he circled the large oak and saw that Mark's arms were still tied at the back of the tree. Everything below Mark's chest was completely gone, and bits of organs hung from his chest cavity. Robby assumed the rib area was as high as the pigs could reach. He checked his surroundings again and fired off another warning shot. He wasn't about to be on that morning's menu.

Shit, I have to pull down the rest of him. I'm not taking any chances that someone would see this once I open up my property to hunting again.

After pulling the flipper knife from his pocket, Robby sawed away at the tape and rope until it unraveled and broke. Mark's upper body dropped to the ground with a thud. Robby leaned over and cut what remained of Mark's shirt off him. He searched the ground as he walked the area and picked up every piece of clothing he could find from both men. He would burn everything in the firepit before heading to Houma.

"Looks like I need to get a move on if I'm going to get to the sheriff's office before nine."

Back at the house, Robby squirted lighter fluid over the clothing he'd tossed into the firepit. With a strike of a stick match against his pants zipper, the tip ignited, and he dropped it on the wet clothes. They burst into flames, and he watched for a few minutes then went to the cooler. After tossing a chunk of meat to Pete, Robby climbed into his truck and drove away.

Chapter 41

When we arrived at the sheriff's office, we found Conway standing in the hallway with two of his deputies.

"Agents DeLeon and Monroe, this is Johnny Whitley and Brian Smythe, two of my weekend deputies who offered to put in a little overtime. They're available to escort you today to wherever you need to go."

We shook hands with the deputies, thanked them, and said we would be ready to head out at nine o'clock.

On my laptop, we pulled up John Cavanaugh's address, or at least the residence that had been in the Cavanaugh family since 1922. It was the only address on record for any Cavanaugh in the parish. I programmed it into my cell phone, and we moved on to Evan Millbrook's address and did the same. I was most curious about John since he lived within a few miles of the dump site that Mark and Billy had discovered.

I looked at Renz. "That reminds me. When do you want Mark, Billy, and Bob to get together?"

"Did I hear someone mention my name?"

I turned toward the door and saw Bob. He walked in and took a seat across from me.

"What's on the schedule for today, Agents?"

"There's a good chance we won't need you until later in the day," Renz said. "We're going to pay some of those people you'd mentioned a visit, and then we have a few folks with misdemeanor records that we'll call on too. We can't take a civilian into a potentially risky situation with us, and yesterday, you'd mentioned not wanting to have anyone think you're a snitch."

Bob chuckled. "There is that. Okay, I'll come back later." He stood to leave.

I walked to the door to let the deputies know we were ready to go. "Sorry to waste your time, Bob, but since you don't have a phone, there was no way to contact you."

"Why is that, anyway?" Renz cocked his head and stared at Bob.

Bob shrugged. "Is there a law that says I need one?"

"Nope. I guess there isn't. Just wondering."

Bob stood his ground and didn't respond.

Conway walked in just as Bob was about to leave. "Hang on, everyone. I have somebody here that you may want to talk to before you head out."

"Who is it?" I asked.

"Billy Bennett's wife. She said he's been gone since yesterday, and she can't reach him on his phone. They had an argument, and he said he had a meeting about some new opportunity and then stormed out. She hasn't seen him since."

I glanced at Renz. "We need to talk to her before we go anywhere." I turned to Conway. "Show her in."

Bob inched out into the hallway. "I better get going, then. I don't want to be a distraction."

I raised my hands. "No, you should stay. You might have something useful to offer." I pointed at the chair he'd been sitting on. "Go ahead and sit back down."

Seconds later, Conway returned with a woman who looked to be in her mid-thirties. She wore her straight blond hair snugged behind her ears with a headband, and without makeup, her bloodshot eyes were more than obvious. She wore shorts and a T-shirt, nothing fancy, and I was sure that her attire was the last thing on her mind.

"Mrs. Bennett." I gave her a nod and pointed at an empty chair. "Have a seat, ma'am."

Conway took the vacant chair next to her.

"Please, just call me Lorna. Can you find my husband?"

She looked frantic, and we needed to calm her to better understand what had happened.

"Take a deep breath, Lorna. How about a cup of coffee? I'd like you to relax a little so we can get all the facts as accurately as possible."

She nodded. "Okay, thank you."

Conway pulled the landline phone across the table to him and called the lobby's desk. "Marie, can you start us a pot of coffee and bring it in here with five cups? Thank you."

He apologized for the interruption, then with a head tip from Renz, I knew it would be my interview.

"Let's just start out with the easy stuff, shall we?" I gave her a reassuring smile. "May I see your driver's license?"

"Sure." She fumbled with her wallet then slipped the ID card out of the sleeve and passed it across the table to me.

I took a picture of it, passed it back, and saw that Renz had his notepad and pen ready to go. Before I began, Marie walked in with a carafe of coffee and five disposable cups. Conway thanked her, and Renz poured the coffee. I went around the table, made the introductions, and when Lorna was ready, I began the questioning.

"Okay, Lorna, walk us through the last thirty-six hours."

"Thirty-six?"

"From Wednesday night. Most people don't realize that problems could have been brewing twelve to twenty-four hours before an argument even happens. Having that information does help. What were you and Billy doing Wednesday night?"

"He went to the LLHC meeting like he does every week."

I frowned. "What does that stand for?"

"Sorry. Lower Louisiana Hunting Club."

I looked at Bob. "Do you belong to that club?"

"Nope. It's a little too pricey for my blood."

Lorna cut in. "Billy gets a reduced membership fee since he's a board member. They have a welcome meeting and cocktail party twice a month for new members."

"And that was Wednesday night?"

"Yes."

"Did you have a problem with him going?"

"Other than the fact that he always comes home drunk, no. I'm used to it."

I gave Renz a glance then turned to Bob. "You and Lorna have never met?"

"No, can't say that we have. Hunting here is predominantly a male sport. Don't really see any ladies out there boar hunting."

"Humph." I looked back at Lorna. "Okay, so what time did Billy come home on Wednesday night?"

Lorna shrugged. "I don't know. I was in bed. He usually comes home, lays on the recliner, watches TV, and falls asleep. Sometimes, he's there all night."

"Got it." I took a sip of coffee and watched her movements. She was fidgety. "Is something other than Billy on your mind?"

"What? No, of course not. I just can't imagine what he meant when he said he had a business opportunity to check out yesterday morning. It was around eight thirty when he left the house, which seems early to me."

"Maybe a breakfast meeting?"

"No, he ate before he left. As usual, he didn't tell me shit, like where he was going, who the meeting was with, or what it was about. I was pissed. It's like I'm just the wife who is only around to cook, clean, rear the kids, and have sex when he says so."

I frowned. "Has Billy ever left for more than a day after an argument?"

"No, and that's why I'm here. He'll go tie one on, come home in the middle of the night, and then we eventually have make-up sex the next day. He never came home yesterday, so I chalked it up to what he normally does, but when he didn't show up last night or this morning, my gut said something was wrong."

"And you tried calling and texting him?"

"Yes, both a dozen times."

"Does Billy keep any guns in his vehicle?"

"No, only when he goes hunting."

"And he has a red Dodge Ram?"

Lorna looked surprised. "How would you know that?"

"We met Billy several days back. He was with Mark LaFleur. You know him, right?"

"Yes. They grew up together and have been pals most of their lives."

"Then maybe Mark knew where Billy was going yesterday morning. Have you called him?"

"I have, and he doesn't pick up either."

Her story was getting stranger by the minute. "Do you know for a fact that all of Billy's guns are accounted for?"

"Well, no. I mean, why would that be the first thing I'd check?"

"Not insinuating anything, Lorna. I'm just covering all the bases. How often does Billy go out hunting?"

"Three times a week, probably, but usually with Mark, and that just wasn't how it appeared yesterday."

Renz spoke up for the first time. "In my mind, even if the business opportunity meeting was in a restaurant, I'd still picture his clothing being business casual or sport jacket attire. How was Billy dressed when he left home?"

Her eyes widened. "That son of a bitch was lying to me. He had on jeans and a long-sleeved plaid shirt."

"Well, it doesn't mean he was lying, but it could mean

the meeting was held outside. Maybe a property purchase, a land agreement, or a new development somewhere he and the person he was meeting had to look at and discuss outdoors. Do you have any investment property?"

"We have two small rental properties. They're the only reason I don't have to work outside the home."

"And what does Billy do for a living?" I asked.

She lowered her voice and her head. "He manages properties."

Renz took over. "Okay, here's my card. We're going to be out interviewing people in an investigation we're working on until midafternoon, I'd assume. I want you to keep trying Billy and Mark, and we'll do the same. If you reach either of them, call me and let me know. Otherwise, come back here at five o'clock today, and we'll come up with a plan of action." Renz turned to Conway. "Why don't you have Lorna fill out the report so it's on file? We'll go over everything with her later, and having that part complete will speed up the process. Meanwhile, I'd suggest putting out a BOLO on Billy's truck and an APB for him."

I asked Lorna a final question. "Is Mark married?"

"No, he's been a lifelong bachelor and lives alone."

"Okay." I passed my phone across the table to her. "Program Billy's and Mark's numbers in there for me. That's the easiest way to go, and we'll be in touch with you throughout the day." I looked at Conway. "Let us know if you get a hit on the BOLO or APB too."

"Sure thing, Agent Monroe." He walked Lorna to his office, and we said goodbye to Bob then left with the deputies.

Chapter 42

It was ten thirty by the time we slowed at the driveway of John Cavanaugh's property. I hoped that meeting would start somewhat smoother than the one with the Duggar's the day before. According to Leroy, John was a batterer, which meant he likely had a bad temper. We were about to see how things played out with two sheriff's deputies and two FBI agents, all armed, arriving at his front door.

Smythe was behind the wheel and seemed like a take-no-prisoners kind of guy. He didn't beat around the bush, and I was sure he would know how to handle just about any type of personality. I was confident that Renz and I could, too, but we were out of our element by a long shot, so having local law enforcement with us was helpful.

Smythe barreled down the long dirt driveway, and like the others, John's home was far closer to the water than it was to the road. We waited for the dust to settle before climbing out of the car, and once it had, we saw a man sitting on a rocker on a long covered porch. He stood, put his hands on his hips, and yelled out that we better have a damn good reason for being there.

Again, as we approached, Renz said he would take the lead.

The man raised his hand. "That's far enough, and I expect an answer before you take another step."

We stopped twenty feet from him, bookended by the deputies, and Renz yelled out.

"We're FBI agents, and we're here with the Terrebonne Parish Sheriff's Office deputies to ask you a few questions. That's if you're John Cavanaugh."

A boy stuck his head around the corner of the house and yelled out. "He's John Cavanaugh, my pa."

John spun. "Riley, get your ass in the house right now and tell your mama that I'll deal with both of you later."

Renz called out to get the man's attention back on us. "The kid didn't mean any harm, sir. May we ask you a few questions about people in the area?"

"Why?"

"We aren't local, that's apparent, but we need information from locals who may know someone who could be capable of abducting people. A handful of young folks have gone missing in the last few months, and some have met with foul play. We're hoping to speak with people who might know of somebody who fits that bill."

"Well, I don't. I mind my own business, and by doing that, I'll probably live a longer life."

"So you don't know anyone like that, or you just don't want to tell us that person's name?"

I discreetly stepped on Renz's toe. He was pushing his luck, and I wanted to walk away in one piece. I'd already come to the conclusion that there wasn't a way to prove or disprove what anyone told us. People could and likely did lie to us, and there was no way to know the difference.

"I don't know any kidnappers, but I wouldn't tell you if I did. Your best bet is to stay out of people's business—for your own good."

"Is that a—"

I cut in before Renz finished the sentence. "Thank you, Mr. Cavanaugh. Have a nice day."

John grabbed the screen door, cursed us out, and disappeared into the house, where I heard him yell Riley's name.

I jerked my head toward the car. "We need to think this through and preferably do it off his property."

Back out on Bayou Dularge Road, Deputy Smythe pulled over, and we got out and talked across the hood of his car.

"What are you thinking, Jade?" Renz asked.

"Nobody is going to be truthful with us. We're wasting our time and chasing our tails, and for what? We're outsiders, have no idea who we're looking for, and also have no idea if anyone will tell us an ounce of truth."

Whitley nodded. "Sorry, Agent DeLeon, but I have to agree with Agent Monroe. These people are never forthright when it comes to talking to the law. That's why we usually just leave them alone. They won't help us—ever."

"Then what about the stories Leroy and Zeke Duggar told us? What about the names they gave us?"

Smythe scratched his head. "In my opinion?"

"Yeah, sure," Renz said.

"It's all bullshit. They say what you want to hear because they want you to leave them alone. If they tell you a good story that you buy hook, line, and sinker, there's a chance you won't come back. That's the end goal—to get you to leave. If I was in charge of the investigation, I'd only deal with reliable people and reliable leads."

"Which we have none of," Renz said.

I took my turn. "I don't know. I think Bob is reliable."

Renz nodded. "Yeah, maybe, and what would he have to gain by lying to us?"

"Nothing, so let's knock out the Evan Millbrook lead and then forget about them. We'll go back to the sheriff's office and see what we can find out about Billy's disappearance."

We headed northwest to Mandalay, and after a round of door knocking and walking Evan Millbrook's property, it appeared that nobody was home. As Smythe drove us back to the sheriff's office, I called Lorna Bennett to ask if she'd heard from Billy. She said she hadn't. I suggested she meet us at the sheriff's office for another question and answer session. I didn't know if Billy's disappearance was related to the murder investigation, but I doubted that it was. Billy was a grown man who could probably handle himself just fine unless he was completely blindsided and ambushed by somebody with a weapon. But without word that someone had a grudge against him, I couldn't understand why anyone would do that.

The deputies dropped us off at the Explorer. Renz and I were going to grab some lunch, and I made the call to

Conway as Renz drove. We agreed to reconvene with Lorna at one o'clock and try to figure out where Billy could be and why nobody could reach Mark LaFleur either.

We sat at a booth inside the typical family-styled restaurant with brass and floral décor. The booths lined the outer walls, and the center of the room was filled with tables. From the number of people bellied up to the tables, I assumed the food was good. We placed our drink orders, mine being sweet tea, and browsed the menu. The grilled chicken breast sandwich, fries, and coleslaw would be fine. Renz said he was going to order two double cheeseburgers and fries.

As Renz sipped his coffee, I talked. "What do you make of Billy Bennett going missing?"

He shrugged. "Don't know yet. We don't really know the guy or his habits, especially when an argument is involved. What strikes me as odd is that Lorna couldn't get in touch with Mark LaFleur either."

I nodded. "I tried his number twice, and both times, it went to voicemail. I think we should stop at his house, bang on the door, and talk to some of the neighbors."

Renz agreed. "We will but not until we get some more answers from Billy's wife."

I was discouraged by our lack of leads. We had nothing that advanced the investigation, and we were on our fifth day in Louisiana. "We're going to go home empty-handed, aren't we?"

"There's a good chance that we will. We're accustomed to neighbors seeing something, cameras catching crimes, and people cooperating with the law. All of those advantages that we're used to are much more challenging when everyone owns twenty acres of land or more."

I rattled my fingers on the table.

Renz frowned. "Something percolating in your brain?"

"All we have are the videos of Carla and the mystery man at Bubba Mike's. The rest, except for the skull identified as Casey Witherspoon's, is probably made-up information, and it's distracting us from finding the actual killer."

Renz sighed. "True enough. So what do you suggest since we only have two days left here?"

"Like Smythe said, work with facts and only facts. Let's eat our lunch and get back to the sheriff's office so we can talk to Lorna, review the footage again, and compile a list of things that we can actually work with."

"So you're saying we should start over?"

"Yep." I rolled my eyes. "That is, unless you have a better idea."

"Humph."

I grinned. "That's what I thought."

Chapter 43

Conway, Lorna, Renz, and I sat around the table in our office. In front of Conway was the missing person's report that Lorna had filled out earlier regarding Billy's disappearance. We had already asked some of the questions, but Billy's height, weight, eye and hair color, identifying features, birthdate and age, and doctor and dentist information were new.

The typical missing person would have been looked into by the sheriff's office and wouldn't concern us. We weren't sent to Houma to investigate missing people, only to find the killer who had already dumped what was left of the victims he'd murdered. But since it was Billy and Mark who had discovered the last known remains, there could be a connection, and we needed to check into that. I was also concerned that nobody had contacted the sheriff's office about Mark, but according to Lorna, Mark's parents had moved to Florida years back, and he had only one sibling, a sister living in New Orleans.

Conway let out a hard breath. "Okay, so what's our focus going to be?"

Renz gave me a head tip, and I began. "We need to know

more about Billy, and then we'll direct our attention to Mark too. We don't know if their disappearances have anything to do with our current investigation, yet it seems awfully coincidental that they're the men who discovered the last dump site, and now they're both unaccounted for."

Conway scratched his head and turned to Lorna. "Okay, we need to know everything. Does Billy have any enemies, anyone who is pissed at him, like a tenant, maybe?"

"No, not to my knowledge. Billy is outgoing and friendly, and most everyone likes him."

Renz took his turn. "He hasn't mentioned a new business opportunity to you in the last week or so? Something that he's been talking to someone about?"

"Nope. Like I said earlier, I'm just the wife. I don't create an income, so I have no say in what he does with our money."

"And the last thing he did before telling you about the so-called business opportunity meeting he was going to was the LLHC meeting the night before."

"Yes. The first I spoke to him about anything was yesterday morning. I got up, made breakfast, he ate, and then he said he was leaving for this alleged meeting. I knew nothing about it, and he'd never mentioned it the day before or any time prior to that."

I tipped my head at her. "Try his phone again and put it on Speaker." We watched as Lorna tapped Billy's name on her phone, set it on the table, and waited as it rang. It immediately went to his outgoing voice message.

Renz piped up. "Does Billy ever turn off his phone?"

Her eyes watered as she spoke. "We fight and argue, Agent DeLeon, but he isn't that mean and spiteful. Our argument was very typical, not a knock-down, drag-out fight. He wouldn't ditch me and the kids and let me worry like that."

I covered her hand with my own. "Okay, try Mark's phone again."

Her results were the same, and it appeared that Mark's phone had been turned off too.

Conway shook his head. "There's something suspicious going on." He looked at Lorna. "And Billy didn't say a word about meeting up with Mark yesterday?"

"Not a word, and when I went back home earlier, I checked Billy's guns—they're all accounted for."

That in itself made me worry. If something had happened to him, Billy didn't have a way to defend himself other than by using his own strength.

I shook my head, and Renz noticed.

"What?"

"If nothing was different and Billy didn't say anything about leaving early yesterday morning for a meeting, then it must have been arranged during the party at the hunting club the night before. That would make sense, wouldn't it?"

"Not a bad conclusion, Jade," Renz said. "Do you know any of the members there, Lorna?"

"Yeah, Mark. Billy and Mark were on the board together."

I palmed my face. "Shit."

Renz pointed at my laptop. "Pull up the club's website

and see what you can find out."

"On it." I slid it over and began tapping the keys. "Okay, on the calendar of events, it shows Wednesday night's new-member-orientation meeting and cocktail party."

"Anything for today or tonight?"

"The budget committee is supposed to meet at seven o'clock tonight."

"Then we'll make sure to be there. We should also find out who those new members were that signed up. There's a good chance that something may have been discussed at the club over cocktails that resulted in Billy's disappearance and possibly Mark's too."

I tipped my chin at Conway. "So nothing yet on the BOLO or APB?"

"Not a peep."

I turned to Lorna. "Do you know what Mark drives?"

"A newer-model silver truck. That's all I can tell you about it."

"Good enough. I'll get more details from the DMV, including the plate number. Meanwhile, we need a list of three of Billy's closest friends or relatives who live in the area."

"The only close friend in the area is Mark. Everyone else is people in the property management field or from the hunting club. They're friends, but I wouldn't consider them close, and Billy doesn't hang out with them. Our nearest relative lives in Baton Rouge."

"All right. Then we'll start with trying to track down Mark. Lorna, I want you to keep calling Billy's phone and then reach out to the other people he knows, including those relatives from Baton Rouge. We need to know if he's mentioned anything to anyone about that business opportunity." I stood. "Come on, Renz. Let's see if there's any action at Mark LaFleur's house."

The DMV listed the vehicle, plate number, and address for Mark LaFleur. With that, we pulled up a copy of his driver's license, which gave us his height, weight, birthdate, and hair and eye color. According to his DMV records, he lived just south of Mechanicville off State Road 57.

The drive there took only ten minutes, but when we arrived, I was even more confused than I was before. Parked in the driveway was the silver Ford F-150 pickup that belonged to Mark. The plates matched the vehicle listed on Mark's DMV records.

I feared the worst. "What the hell? Maybe something happened inside the house."

Renz leapt from the Explorer and banged on Mark's door. I caught up, cupped my hands around my face, and peered in the front window. The lights were off, and all I could see was the living room and part of the kitchen.

"I'll check the back."

"Hold up," Renz said. "We'll go together." As we passed the truck, Renz felt the hood then shook his head. "Hasn't been driven lately. The engine is cold."

The house wasn't fenced in, and as we crossed into the backyard, a neighbor called out to us.

"Can I help you?"

"We're looking for Mark LaFleur. Have you seen him?" I asked.

"Who's asking?"

We didn't have time for everyone who was suspicious of our behavior. I pulled out my badge and held it toward him so he could see it clearly. "We're the FBI, and we need to speak with Mark. Do you know where he is?"

"I haven't seen him since early Wednesday evening when he left for the hunting club. The truck has been parked in the same spot ever since."

"Are you a close friend?"

The man shrugged. "I'm Scott, and we're just neighbors. We shoot the shit now and then, but I wouldn't say we're buddies."

"So you don't have a key to his house?" I asked.

"No, ma'am, I sure don't."

"Okay, thanks." I continued on and looked through the slider while Renz peered through the higher bedroom windows. "I don't see anything, Renz."

"We still need to go inside to make sure he isn't lying in a room that we can't see."

"I agree. Want to try the slider?"

"Yep, let's tackle that first."

We stood side by side with open hands pressed against the slider. On Renz's go, we pushed up on the glass, lifted it out of the track, and forced the lock to release the door. We were in. Renz called out Mark's name several times but didn't get a response. We searched every room and the garage, and found nobody home. There weren't signs of a break-in or foul play. Mark wasn't there.

"I don't get it. He isn't here, I don't see a cell phone or

keys lying around, but his truck is outside."

"Right, so that means he took his phone and keys and either left with someone in a different vehicle or went somewhere on foot."

I wiped the sweat from my forehead as we walked outside. "I'm not buying a story of him going anywhere on foot in ninety-plus-degree weather and nearly as much humidity. No way, no how." I walked to the truck and pulled the door handle. It was locked. "The truck is only a year old, so I doubt if anything is wrong with it. My bet is on Mark leaving with someone else. If he went to the hunting club Wednesday night but came back home and parked here, and hasn't been seen since, my guess is that Billy picked him up. Just because Lorna didn't know about it doesn't mean it didn't happen."

Renz leaned against the bed of the truck. "I've got to agree with you. It's the only thing that makes sense."

I looked down the street. "So if Billy picked him up, that means Mark's house was on the way to wherever they went. My gut says they headed south since Billy lives north of here. He offered to pick up Mark on the way, and they drove to that location together."

"What are you doing?" Renz looked at me as I crossed the lawn to the neighbor's house.

"I'm going to ask that curious neighbor if he saw a red truck stop here yesterday morning and pick up Mark."

"Great idea, but wait up. There might be more questions worth asking."

Chapter 44

Robby had been driving around aimlessly as he waited to go back to the sheriff's office.

Damn it, there's no sense in wasting gas.

He turned in at the drive-through lane of a hamburger joint, placed his order, paid, and found a shaded picnic table in a park to sit at while he ate his meal. Robby pondered the meeting the agents had with Lorna Bennett. He replayed the questions they'd asked her as well as the ones they'd asked him. They knew about the hunting club, and even though Robby had used his real name when he joined, that didn't mean the agents wouldn't go there and snoop around for information. Things could get dicey, and he needed to be careful.

The fact that Billy and Mark had literally been devoured—and that what remained of their clothing had been burned in the firepit—gave Robby little reason to worry about becoming a suspect unless the agents learned that everything he'd said about himself was a lie.

And that's only if they come up with a reason to look my way.

Robby was getting bored. Killing Mark and Billy was an escape from his dull life, but since he didn't have much of a hand in their actual deaths and they didn't fill his cooler, he was itching to get back in the game. Emptying people's pockets of their hard-earned cash was a necessary evil for him to stay afloat. It also kept gas in his truck so he could scout around for his next victim.

He wiped the ketchup from his chin and licked his finger. When he heard an argument between a man and woman in a car parked in the last space nearest the street, he turned. Robby watched with interest as the fight intensified. The woman leapt from the car, slammed the door, and took to the sidewalk with her purse slung over her shoulder.

Hmm, she looks good in those pink shorts and halter top.

Robby quickly tossed his trash, returned to the truck, and watched. He was ready to go if an opportunity arose. The man squealed the tires as he pulled out onto the street and slowed alongside the woman. More words were exchanged, and she gave him the middle finger and continued on. That was Robby's cue. He turned the key in the ignition and drove to the end of the lot. The timing was right. The man yelled a few curse words then sped off. The woman was fair game, and just as Robby rolled up on her, she stuck out her thumb to indicate she was looking for a ride.

Perfect, just perfect.

Robby slowed to a stop, leaned over, and rolled down the passenger-side window. "What seems to be the problem, hon?"

"Damn boyfriend, that's the problem! We fought, I got out of the car, and after cussing me out, he drove away."

"Where ya going?"

"Just a few miles south to Mulberry."

"Really? That's on my way home. I live in Sunshine, so we're damn near neighbors. Want a ride?"

"Hell yeah. I'll show that asshole I don't need him."

Robby chuckled. "That's the spirit. Hop on in."

His mind was racing. The only way to make her compliant was with a fast punch to the head. His heart pounded double time. He could barely contain himself as he imagined her tied to his victim tree. He would watch her succumb to the elements and maybe let a gator nibble her toes before he slit her throat and hung her upside down to bleed out. She was young, and her meat would be tender. He nearly salivated at the thought. Robby was sure she'd have something in that purse of hers that he could use too.

"So, neighbor, what's your name?"

She grinned, and her teeth glistened. He planned to knock them down her throat soon enough. "My name is Sally. How about you?"

"I'm Troy."

"Nice name. Like one of those Greek gods or something, right?"

Robby knew just enough about history to sound smart. "Troy was a city in Asia Minor, which in today's world is Turkey, but yeah, that's close enough."

"Cool."

"So do you live with your folks, Sally?"

"My ma. My pop died in a boating accident three years ago back on Forbidden Bayou." She shook her head. "That area is cursed something bad, and they never found his body—just the empty boat that had strangely taken on water, yet there weren't any holes in it to cause it to leak. Local folks say the gators probably got him."

"Could be true. Gators like meat, and they aren't picky as to where it came from. But then again, it could be those swamp people who practice voodoo and use Satan's serpents during their sacrificial rituals back in the bayou."

She shivered. "Those folklore stories give me the willies."

"Don't know how much folklore is involved. I'd venture to say they're all true."

Robby had just passed the last commercial building in Houma on his way out of town. Flat country, canals, and farther back, the swamps were all that lay between the small towns along Bayou Dularge Road.

"What do you do for work, Troy?"

"I bartend."

She giggled. "I love to drink, but my ma frowns on it. Says Jesus doesn't approve."

Robby flashed her a huge smile. "Open the glove box, honey. I've got a bottle of whiskey in there, and I approve."

She bounced up and down on the seat. "Really? I can have some?"

"Damn straight." He pointed at her. "You and me? We're gonna party."

Sally pushed the button, and the glove box door fell open. Robby's opportunity came the very second that she dipped her head to peer in. He reached across the seat, grabbed her by the neck, and smashed her face into the dash three times until she slumped against the door. He checked the mirrors, didn't see another vehicle in sight, and screeched to a stop. With a handful of her hair, Robby yanked her across the seat, and with all his might, he smashed her head into the dash one final time. She was out for the count and probably had a good concussion too. He would have her tied to the tree before she regained consciousness.

Chapter 45

I was disappointed that we hadn't learned much about Mark from Scott. He said he had seen Mark Thursday morning through the living room window when Mark went outside to get the daily newspaper. Scott said he made a cup of coffee then went to his home office, where he worked for hours after that. He hadn't seen Mark since.

After thanking him and leaving, we confirmed that Friday morning's paper was still in the tube holder, and the mailbox had enough mail in it to make us believe it hadn't been retrieved since Wednesday.

We checked with several other neighbors, but most said they had been at work at that time of morning. Discouraged, I climbed into the passenger seat of the Explorer, and we headed to the sheriff's office. The one thing we were certain of was that Billy had picked up Mark yesterday morning before they left for destinations unknown. Neither had been seen or spoken to since.

I looked at Renz as he drove. "This has to be related to the investigation."

He tapped his fingers against the steering wheel. I

assumed it was his way of processing what we did and didn't know.

Renz finally spoke. "The only way those two would be a target is if the killer knew they were the guys who found the remains."

"But so what? That doesn't mean *they* knew who the killer was." I stared at Renz and waited for an answer.

"They must have told everyone they knew about the discovery," he said.

"So you're saying somebody they told is the killer?"

"There's a high likelihood of it."

My skin crawled at the thought. "Damn it. Billy and Mark may have caused their own abduction if that's what really happened." I shook my head in disbelief. "How is that even possible, though?"

Renz frowned. "In what way?"

"Physically. How could one person overtake two men?"

"By blindsiding them. Either the killer followed them yesterday to that business meeting and ambushed them, or—"

"Or what?"

"Or the business meeting they went to was with the killer and they didn't know it."

My head was spinning. "Do you actually think they're dead?"

"I don't know, but I'm guessing there's a good chance they are. I also think if the killer knows that law enforcement is closing in, nobody will ever find Billy or Mark's bones."

I stared out the window and watched as the wetlands

passed by. I wondered how many secrets lay hidden in those bayous, and I wasn't sure I would ever find out.

"Are we going to tell Lorna of our suspicions?"

Renz raked his hair. "Not yet. We need to talk to the board members from the hunting club tonight. I want an account of everything they remember and everyone they spoke to Wednesday night. We also need to review the applications submitted by the new members."

I checked the time on the infotainment center. We had three hours before the meeting was scheduled to begin. "Let's tell Lorna that Mark wasn't home but his truck was in the driveway. We can't say for sure that he was with Billy yesterday, but it's the only thing that makes sense."

Renz nodded. "And it's all we have right now."

We returned to the sheriff's office, updated Conway, and spoke to Lorna. She was tasked with contacting everyone Billy knew, even casual acquaintances. According to what she'd learned, nobody had spoken to him or knew about that business opportunity he was going to check out. If speaking to members at the hunting club didn't give us new information, I was afraid the secrets of the bayou murders would remain hidden forever.

Bob arrived a half hour after we got back. "Have any luck with your interviews today?"

Renz looked irritated. "No."

"How about Billy?" Bob turned to Lorna. "Has he come home?"

"That's also a no," Renz said. "You told us you know Billy and Mark."

"Yep, that's true."

"When did you see either of them last?"

Bob scratched his cheek. "A month or so back, I imagine. Came across Billy at the big-box store on the west edge of town." He scratched his cheek again. "Can't remember when I saw Mark last. I gave them hunting tips and advice, but it's not like we hang in the same crowds."

"Humph. That doesn't help. How about their favorite hunting locations?"

"Depends. Hunting wild pigs is legal year round in Louisiana as long as that person holds a valid state hunting license. Boars are everywhere, in all our sixty-four parishes, so I guess if one area has been cleared out, then a hunter would move elsewhere."

"So you're saying you don't know?"

"I know where I like to hunt, but I can't speak for the thousands of other hunters in our state, Agent DeLeon. Why would his favorite hunting spots have anything to do with Billy being missing? I thought he went to a business meeting."

"Just asking. Do you know any of the members in that hunting club, Bob?"

"Other than Billy and Mark, no. Like I said earlier, membership there is too rich for my blood."

I stared at Renz until he looked my way, then I gave him the eyeballs. I couldn't understand why he was being so combative with Bob. The guy had been trying to help us from day one.

"After tomorrow, we won't need your help any longer,

Bob. Looks like we're about to pack it up if we don't track down the killer by Sunday."

"Like I said, I'm a good tracker, but going in on trampled and contaminated ground doesn't work. I don't know if anyone told you about all the venomous snakes in Louisiana. We have rattlers, water moccasins, and now all sorts of pythons from those damn voodoo people back in the Forbidden Bayou."

"That's the second time I've heard that term. Is it a real place?"

Bob chuckled. "Damn straight it is, Jade, but not a place where city folks should wander into. You'd die out there, sure as I'm standing here. Gators, snakes, wild pigs, venomous spiders—they're all in the swamps. Even pig hunters should watch every move they make. Maybe Billy decided to go hunting after that meeting and met up with a critter that got the best of him."

Lorna chimed in. "I counted Billy's guns earlier, and they're all accounted for."

"Sorry, ma'am, I was just thinking out loud."

I checked the time. "We're going to the hunting club soon. We need to take a look at that new-member roster and ask if anyone there knew of that business meeting."

"Well, I hope you find out something, but if not, there's always Beauregard Rue as a last-ditch effort," Bob said.

"Who the hell is Beauregard Rue?" I asked.

"He's the real deal, a true swamper who knows everything that goes on in Terrebonne Parish. If word gets around, it goes through that man first."

"Then why didn't you tell us about him before?" I asked.

"Because you won't get within a mile of his home without his okay. He won't let you on his property unless I'm with you, and I need his permission to bring you in."

Renz huffed. "And what makes you so special?"

"I saved him from the jaws of a gator years back, and that's what makes me special. We're connected."

"When can you talk to him?" I asked.

"Jade, we don't need to get sidetracked with unreliable sources. Let's see if anything pans out at the hunting club, and then you and I will discuss it later," Renz said.

"Okay, fair enough." I turned to Bob. "But can you clear it with him just in case so we aren't wasting time?"

Bob smiled. "I'll see what I can do."

Chapter 46

Renz and I sat in the parking lot at the hunting club and waited for the first car to show up. It was six thirty, and the budget committee meeting was scheduled to begin at seven. Seconds later, two more cars arrived.

"Let's go introduce ourselves and tell them why we're here," Renz said.

We climbed out of the Explorer and approached the men, who were walking toward the building together.

Renz called out. "Excuse us."

The men turned around and waited for us to catch up. We already had our credentials out.

Renz made the introductions and asked who was in charge.

A man named Travis Coltrane spoke up. "We all have equal status here, just different roles. What can we help you with, Agents?"

Renz tipped his head toward the building. "Let's talk inside."

Coltrane opened the door and led the way down the hall. We passed the room where their budget committee meeting was to be held, and folders sat on the table and a whiteboard sat on an easel near the back wall. We continued on, turned right at the end of the hall, and entered what looked to be a banquet room.

"We can talk in here," Coltrane said. "This is where we hold our new-member presentation videos and parties."

"Speaking of new members, we'll need to see who signed up Wednesday night."

"May I ask what this is about?" Coltrane asked.

The men sat and offered us the seats across from them, then I explained our concerns.

"Are Billy Bennett and Mark LaFleur part of your budget committee?"

Donald Bales spoke up. "Yep, and I'm sure they'll be here any minute."

"That's highly unlikely, sir," I said. "It appears that both Billy and Mark have gone missing."

"What? How, when?"

"That's what we're investigating," Renz said. "We believe their disappearance is related to a case we were called into Louisiana to work."

Coltrane looked from Renz to me. "And what is that?"

I wasn't sure Renz wanted everyone in Houma to know about the human remains that had been discovered in several locations throughout the parish, so I kept quiet and allowed him to field the question. He gave me a quick glance before speaking.

"On Monday, Billy and Mark discovered human bones while they were hog hunting off Bayou Dularge Road. They must have discussed that incident with people they knew, and now they're missing and have been since yesterday morning. My question, because they were both here Wednesday night, is if they discussed what they found with any of you before or during the new-member cocktail party?"

Bales responded. "We all knew about it, and there was quite a buzz going on at the club that night. I doubt if it was because we had a half dozen new members."

Renz continued. "Did any of you hear about a business meeting Billy was going to yesterday morning?"

The men looked at each other and shrugged.

"I don't think so. At least I didn't hear anything," Coltrane said.

The other men replied the same way.

"Okay, then how about a look at the new-member applications? Maybe one of those guys brought up an opportunity at the cocktail party."

"Sure, I'll make copies," Don said. "I'll tell the other guys that the budget meeting is going to be delayed for a bit too."

Don returned within five minutes and took his seat. He passed five sheets of paper across the table to us, and I picked them up and flipped through them.

"So you have five new members as of Wednesday night. Were any of them men you knew before they joined?"

Coltrane answered. "Only Drew Moore. The others were strangers."

"Okay, and it looks like their names and addresses are included too. That should help."

"Can you keep us informed, Agents? We'd sure hate to hear that something serious happened to Billy and Mark."

I gave him a nod as I stood but knew it was too late. Something bad had happened all right, that was evident, and we needed to find out what that was and who was responsible. We thanked them and left.

"I'm beat," Renz said as he drove to the hotel. "Let's have supper and call it a day. Taft wants an update, and I'm sure I'll be on the phone with her for a while."

I was fine with that. I wanted to check into those new members first thing tomorrow then find out if Bob had gotten the okay for us to interview Beauregard Rue, but from the way Renz sounded earlier, he wasn't on board and likely thought the man was an old geezer with nothing verifiable to say.

We had supper in the hotel's restaurant then said our good nights at my door. After a much-needed shower to wash the day's humidity off my body, I crawled into bed and searched the name Beauregard Rue on my laptop. Nothing came up. I did the same for Robert Hebert and found hundreds of entries throughout the state. With a groan, I shut down my computer and plugged it in for the night then made my evening call to Amber.

Chapter 47

After the Explorer was parked in the hotel's lot, Robby watched the two agents enter the building. He assumed they were done snooping around for the night. He wondered how it went at the hunting club and didn't feel at all good when he saw Jade walk out with sheets of paper in hand.

Stupid bitch probably has copies of the new-member applications. Hopefully, the name Robert Williams of Dulac means nothing to them, but I have a feeling they'll come calling.

Robby turned the key in the ignition and aimed the headlights for home. He grinned and anticipated a night filled with beer and cheap entertainment. After all, Sally was hanging out there. He laughed at the irony of it, and he was sure the water in the trough had to be near the boiling point by then.

It was ten o'clock by the time Robby turned onto his narrow gravel driveway. The truck jarred him as it bounced and hit every pothole of the half-mile drive. He cut the engine and parked, then he peered out the windshield with the headlights pointed at the victim tree. He smiled when he saw Sally. Blood, long since dried, covered her face from where it had been pummeled against the truck's dashboard. He grabbed his flashlight from the glove box and climbed out then walked to her. Robby shined the light in her face, and although her eyes were swollen closed, she still squinted from the light.

"Enjoying the night, Sally? It sure is nice out with the crickets chirping and owls hooting. I have a hot bath prepared for you. That has to sound good, right?"

She tried to scream, but with tape covering her mouth, her efforts were useless.

"I have two hundred acres of wilderness and swamps back here. There's nobody within miles that can hear you."

She struggled against the ropes, tearing her skin in the process.

"You know gators can smell blood. There's all kinds of venomous snakes out here, too, so if I were you, I'd try to stay as inconspicuous as possible. That is, unless you want to be eaten alive. Truth be told, I'd rather fill my cooler than let the wildlife have you, so settle your ass down."

Robby walked away to check the water in the trough.

Son of a bitch, the fire went out, and the water isn't even hot.

He looked back at her and made up his mind.

What the hell. I'd rather deal with her in the daylight than mess around now when I can't see if sneaky critters are getting too close.

He yelled back as he headed to the house. "Consider this your lucky night. You're going to live to see another sunrise." Robby climbed the stairs and went inside. He would have an early morning if he wanted to kill and process Sally before the agents arrived, but he would do his best to convince Jade to come alone.

Hours passed, and Pete's barking wakened him from a dead sleep. That was definitely unusual. Robby sprang out of bed, fumbled in the dark for the flashlight he'd left on the crate near the front door, and turned it on.

"What are you barking about, Pete?"

Robby peered out the window that faced the driveway. He didn't see any headlights. The sky was just beginning to lighten up to where he could make out the shapes of the trees that surrounded his house. He grumbled as he put on his shoes. Pete scratched at the door. Something was going on outside, and it unnerved Robby. A gator had likely made its way to Sally or farther. It could be anywhere, and Robby didn't want to deal with the gator lunging at him as he walked the yard.

Maybe I should wait another half hour. The sun will be up, and I'll be able to see without the flashlight.

Robby pulled a chair to the window and took a seat. He watched the driveway and waited for daylight. If anyone was sneaking up on him, he planned to be ready. His rifle was only a foot away.

The dog's constant growling and barking told Robby that something or someone was near, but he wasn't about to risk his life to find out what it was. It would either wander off or be shot as soon as Robby got a bead on it through his scope.

As he waited, he thought about Jade Monroe and how

to disable her. She carried her gun everywhere she went, and Robby didn't want to end up on the business end of that barrel. He would have to blindside her, just like he did with everyone else. He would take her into the house, pretending that Beau was waiting for them, then club her into unconsciousness. Killing and cooking a federal agent would be a great accomplishment, but getting away with it would be even better.

Robby glanced at the alarm clock on the windowsill. It was a few minutes before six and light enough outside for him to see what the problem was. He took his rifle and Pete and headed out the door and down the stairs to the yard. He steered clear of the stilted area under the house where the shade made it too dark to see. A gator could be lurking there. Robby walked out to the yard and glanced at the tree where Sally was tied. He squinted—his eyes had to be playing tricks on him. She wasn't there. He spun, looked again, and scanned the yard. There was nobody in sight.

"No, no, no! She couldn't have gotten away. No way in hell!"

He ran to the tree, hoping that if nothing else, a gator had ripped her apart and eaten her, but he didn't find any blood or remnants of clothing. She was just gone. Strands of rope were snagged in the tree bark, and he cursed his bad luck.

"She freed herself? You've got to be kidding!"

Robby ran through the yard, searched the area where the swamp met the ground, then checked the outbuildings—nothing. Her escape was likely why Pete had been barking.

Sally had found a way to get loose and wandered around in the dark. She was gone, and as soon as she hit the road and flagged down a passerby, Robby would be screwed. There was also the chance that somebody had already picked her up. He ran along the water's edge again and into the woods, where he found a muddy shoe. Robby knelt and picked it up. He looked out into the woods as far as he could see then toward the water. No movement caught his eye.

"She can't get far with only one shoe, and if she steps on a snake, she's a goner."

He returned to the house, grabbed his keys, and headed for his truck. If he saw her on the road, he'd hit her, toss her into the back, and finish her off at home. Finding her was more important than anything else at that moment. Robby looked both ways at the end of the driveway. Going left would take Sally deeper into bayou country that was far less civilized, and going right would lead her into Dulac. He had to go right. If she'd actually made it to the road, it was five more miles before she would reach the gas station on the south edge of town. Robby spun the tires and kicked up gravel as he turned right out of the driveway. He had to drive slowly and watch out the passenger-side window into the swampland. If Sally was still wandering through the woods, he would see her making her way to the road. If she'd reached the road, that would be her safety net unless Robby found her first. But if she was headed deeper into the swamps and waterways, that would surely lead to her death.

He spent the next hour driving back and forth down a two-mile stretch of Four Point Road. Robby doubted that she could have gotten farther than that, especially when she had to find her way out of the swamp first.

Maybe a gator or a snake got her and I'm worrying for nothing. Someone as stupid as her and with only one shoe on probably wouldn't even know which direction the road was.

After finally giving up, Robby headed home and decided to track her movements through the swamp instead. It was probably the only way to find her, and if and when he did, she would be in a world of hurt.

Back at the shack, he grabbed his pistol and headed into the brush where he'd found the shoe more than an hour earlier. Robby spotted her footsteps in the muddy undergrowth and began following them. Luckily, she'd headed opposite the road and deeper into the swamp. A half hour and dozens of mosquito bites later, he saw evidence of what could have been a scuffle along the banks of the bayou. It appeared that she might have slipped in the mud and slid into the alligator-infested waters. The ground was torn up, and Robby saw a strip of pink material. He remembered her shorts being pink.

Good, the gators must have sunk their teeth into her after all. Now to get back home, clean up, and head to Houma. Today will be a day to remember.

Chapter 48

It was eight thirty, and Renz and I had just arrived at the sheriff's office with our drive-through breakfast and large coffees. We had to forego the Continental breakfast at the hotel since there was an issue with the refrigeration unit and the breakfast room was closed.

Conway gave the half-opened door a rap. I looked up and waved him in.

"Anything come to light from the hunting club?" he asked.

"We've got the new-member names to check out today, but as far as anyone knowing what happened to Billy or Mark, nope. Nobody heard whispers of a business opportunity meeting Billy was going to Thursday morning either."

"What's happening on the local front? Anything we should worry about?" Renz asked.

He swatted the air. "Not really. Just a squabble between a boyfriend and girlfriend out at Zimmerman Park yesterday and now the boyfriend can't reach her."

I frowned. "If he was a jackass to her, I wouldn't want to be reached either."

Conway shrugged. "Unless she actually comes up missing, I'm leaving it to the boyfriend to track her down. It was their fight, and we can't intervene in every argument between couples."

Renz agreed with a huff. "True enough, and you'd never get anything accomplished if you did."

After pulling my laptop from my briefcase, I set it up. "So, we're checking out the new members at the hunting club, and then?"

"Then hope one of them has a record that we'll dig further into."

I rubbed my chin as I thought. "They couldn't own a firearm if they had a felony record, and why would anyone pay a five-thousand-dollar membership fee if they didn't own a gun?"

Renz sighed. "And it isn't the norm for someone with a misdemeanor record to advance to murder. Let's just check the names one at a time, see if any of them have records, and decide after that."

"I'd still like to have a talk with Beauregard Rue." I waited for a response and tried to read Renz's expression.

He finally spoke up. "If you really want to go, then you should, but I'm not wasting my time. Personally, I think Bob is also a waste of time, but that's just my opinion. If you do go, take a deputy along, and I'll have a deputy help me on this end with interviewing the club members if it seems warranted."

I was pleasantly surprised that Renz didn't flat-out say no, but knocking that off the to-do list was important.

Either the man wouldn't have anything worthwhile to tell me or we could get a real lead that we wouldn't have known about otherwise. No matter what, I was intrigued.

"I promise I won't waste time there, Renz. I'll see if he knows anything that could be helpful and then leave. We've only got one more day here, and then we have to let it go unless something pops. Honestly, between today and tomorrow, that isn't a lot of time."

"Yeah, okay. Maybe splitting up and getting double the work done isn't the worst idea."

I thanked Renz then turned to Conway. "Do you have a deputy I can use for a few hours?"

"Yep, I'll go find somebody for you."

Seconds later, there was another knock on the door—it was Bob.

"Morning, Agents."

I smiled. "You seem chipper today."

"Chipper enough, I guess. The sun is shining, the humidity is down, and Beauregard Rue said he'd allow one person to come onto his property with me."

Renz tapped his pen against the table. "Tell me something, Bob."

"Sure thing, Agent DeLeon."

"Why are people here so skittish around law enforcement?"

"Hmm, guess I haven't given that much thought. There's no particular reason, aimed at police, I mean. People just like their privacy. Folks around here are kind and helpful to one another. We're like one big family, but outsiders cause their antennas to go up. It doesn't matter if you're a cop or a traveling salesman, locals are just suspicious of strangers—stranger danger, remember? If you lived here, you'd see people in a different light."

Renz blew out a huff. "I suppose. It's been a weird year all around."

"So, when do you want to go, and who is that person going to be?"

"Not me," Renz said. "I've got other folks to talk to."

Bob turned to me. "Then it looks like it's you and me, Jade."

"She isn't going anywhere without an escort. Conway is tasking a deputy to go along."

"Um—"

"It's either that or she doesn't go."

"Sure, but there isn't enough room in my truck for three."

"The deputy can follow you in his squad car, and then Jade can ride back with him."

"Yep, okay, but I'll have to clear it with Beau when we get there. I hope it won't be a problem."

Conway returned minutes later and gave Bob a nod. "Mr. Hebert."

Bob returned the greeting. "Sheriff Conway."

I stood. "Guess we can go now unless you need help with those club members first."

"Nah, I'm good. I'll run the names through the system and then interview the ones that I deem necessary. Conway can find someone to help me, but let me know when you're headed back. We'll meet up then."

"You bet." I turned to Bob. "I guess we're good to go."

"I guarantee you it's going to be exciting."

I walked out with Bob and climbed into his truck. Stillman pulled up behind us, lowered his window, and gave us a thumbs-up.

"Looks like he's ready," I said. "Where does Beauregard live?"

"Just outside Dulac, about a half hour south." Bob grinned. "So you may as well sit back and enjoy the ride."

I lowered the window just enough to feel the warm wind on my face. I closed my eyes, hoped for answers, and couldn't wait to get there.

Chapter 49

Robby slowed to a stop beneath the tree canopy and nudged Jade. She woke, looked around, and saw that the truck was idling on a driveway. "I must have dozed off. Are we here?"

"Yep. I'm going to jump out and have a quick talk with the deputy. He'll have to wait down here unless Beau says it's okay for him to join us. Give me just a minute, and then we'll go on up, find out, and if it's okay, I'll come back and let him know."

"All right. I'll need a minute to wake up and get my bearings, anyway."

Robby climbed out and walked to the squad car twenty feet behind his truck. He glanced back and saw Jade looking straight ahead. He lifted the flipper knife from his pocket and cupped it in his hand.

Stillman lowered his window as Robby approached. The sun peeking through the trees was angled right in Stillman's face. He shielded his eyes and waited. "What's going on?"

Robby lowered his head and leaned in. "You'll have to wait here until I get approval from the resident for you to join us."

"Okay, not a problem."

"This might be, though." It took only a split second for Robby to bury the blade up to the handle into the deputy's neck. Robby backed away for a second so the initial blood pumping from the deputy's artery wouldn't spray on his clothing or hands. He reached in and grabbed Stillman by the hair. Robby pulled the deputy's head back and slit his throat, then he gave him a push toward the console and watched as he slumped into unconsciousness.

"You'll be dead in a minute or two, so I guess we're good." He pocketed the bloody knife after wiping it on the deputy's sleeve. Robby ripped out the radio, raised the window, pulled out the keys, and walked back to the truck. He tossed the keys into the brush before climbing in.

"Everything okay?"

"Yep, and Stillman has no problem with us going in ahead of him."

"Good. I'm excited."

"Me too." Robby continued on. "The stilt house is about another quarter mile in. There's a lot of potholes in this driveway, too, so you might get bounced around."

"Just part of the charisma of the bayou life, right?"

"You bet." At the end of the driveway, Robby parked near the firepit and killed the engine. He dropped the keys into his pocket, rounded the front of the truck, and opened Jade's door. "This is the place, Agent Monroe."

She looked around and took in everything. "What's with the big kettle of water over the coals?"

Robby shrugged. "Beau cooks his game outside. Maybe

he's planning to boil something later."

"Got it. So a stilt house, a few sheds, and then farther back, the bayou?"

"Pretty much, and not a lot different than most setups near the water. Stilt houses serve several purposes, to be close to the water but up higher in case the waterways flood or a critter comes calling." He noticed Jade shiver.

"That totally freaks me out."

"And so it should. Do you have any idea what the most dangerous predator is?"

"In this environment, I'd say a gator."

"Nope. It's always a human being no matter where you are."

She chuckled. "You got me on that one, Bob. So where is Mr. Rue?"

"Likely inside." Robby jerked his chin toward the steps. "Shall we?"

"Yes, and I'm excited to meet him."

Robby followed Jade up the stairs. He was only inches from her holstered gun, but he couldn't make a move on her until he was on level ground. Chances were, if he attempted to grab it, she would kick him down the flight of stairs. They reached the landing, and Robby pulled open the screen door and called out to the imaginary Beauregard as he motioned for Jade to enter.

She stepped inside and scanned the room then turned to meet a fist to the face. Jade stumbled backward and tried to go for her weapon. Robby moved in fast and clocked her again, that time knocking her to the floor. He straddled her and pinned her arms with his knees.

"Think you're going somewhere, Agent Monroe? Well, think again." Robby pulled her gun from the holster and tucked it in his waistband. Jade moaned and tried to lift her head. She looked up as another blow hit her in the face.

With his hands grasping her wrists, Robby pulled her down the stairs. Her body thumped as it hit each wooden step. He dragged her to the tree where fragments of rope still remained from Sally's escape. Using them, he secured Jade's wrists behind her back and her ankles together, then he ran to the shed for more rope, nails, and a hammer. She was already squirming to free herself when he returned.

"Bob, what in God's name are you doing? Are you insane?"

"Maybe, but this is what I do, and I enjoy every second of it. It makes me feel alive by feeding my body and paying my bills. There isn't a Beauregard Rue. I made him up to lure you here. Mark and Billy are dead and have been devoured by the wild pigs, but that's okay. My personal tastes lean more toward the ladies, anyway." Robby knelt at her side, licked his lips, and whispered, "You'll be far more tender and tasty."

"You sick son of a bitch. It was you all along, and you wormed your way into our investigation so you could stay on top of our progress. It was you who flattened my tire at the fast-food restaurant."

Robby laughed. "Ding, ding, ding. You win a gold star for having an average IQ. Now, let's get this tree set up again."

As she lay face down in the dirt, Jade turned her head to see what he was doing. The trunk of the tree only a few feet away was covered in a deep red tint, and the ground beneath it looked the same.

"Oh my God."

"Yep, this here is the victim tree." Robby patted it proudly. "It's where the killings take place most of the time, except in Mark and Billy's case. I don't want the boars coming close to the house. It could get dangerous, so I took care of them back in the woods. After I slice an artery, I string up the body to bleed out, gut them, strip the meat from the bones, and toss that meat in the trough of boiling water. Within hours, I have enough protein to hold me over for weeks."

Robby pounded a half dozen nails into the tree, bent them over, and ran the rope through several times. He secured the ends to the rope Jade was already bound with then pulled her to the tree and stood her in an upright position.

"I'm actually getting proficient at this, except something went wrong yesterday and my latest guest, Sally, got away. Signs back in the swamp make it appear that a gator found her, though, so she's out of the picture. I guess I got careless when I tied her up since my mind was on you, Jade. You're going to be my trophy kill."

Jade spewed blood from her mouth as she yelled. "Not if I can help it, asshole!"

Robby chuckled. "As if you're in any position to threaten me. Maybe you haven't noticed yet, but you're tied to a damn tree. I'll be back soon, but right now, I need to get a fire started."

"Deputy Stillman will wonder why this meeting is taking so long. He'll come to investigate, or he'll call Conway."

"Not happening, Jade. Stillman is dead. I slit his throat, ripped his radio from the car, and tossed the keys in the bushes. Nobody is looking for you, and they wouldn't know where to find you, anyway. Every bit of information I gave you and DeLeon was fake, including where I live and my name. Hell, I'm not even married, and I don't have any kids. I'm a ghost to you and to the sheriff's office, so good luck tracking me down. Oh, and in case you're wondering, I turned off your phone and tossed it in the water. Some pea-brained gator probably thought it was food and ate it."

"So it was you who killed all those missing people?"

"Yep, and pretty soon, you'll be added to that total." Robby rubbed his chin. "That probably makes a dozen by now over the years. Had to quit for a while because I messed up my back, but now, I'm as good as new and stronger than ever." He held up his hand to end the conversation. "Enough chatting already. I have a fire to build."

Chapter 50

Renz checked his watch for the fifth time. It was pushing eleven o'clock, and Jade hadn't called him yet. He and Deputy Holbrook didn't find anyone at the home of the only person who had a police jacket. The man's one offense was selling marijuana seven years prior, and he'd stayed out of trouble since then. They returned to the sheriff's office, where Renz knocked on Conway's office door.

"Agent DeLeon, back already?"

"There was only one man who had a police record, and the offense was minor. I'm grasping at straws here." He pointed his thumb over his shoulder. "I'll be plugging away in the office to see if I can come up with anything else."

"Sure thing."

Renz patted the doorframe to leave then turned back. "By the way, has Stillman given you an update from the Rue house?"

Conway cocked his head. "Actually, he hasn't." He tipped his wrist. "They've been gone a few hours, haven't they?"

"Yeah, and that concerns me."

Conway chuckled. "Well, I do know how those old swampers like to bs."

"I thought they shied away from strangers."

"Stillman isn't a stranger to them. That's why I chose him to go along with Agent Monroe. His granddad was a gator hunter and has lived out in the bayous his whole life. The man is ninety years old but still likes to throw back a beer and shoot the shit."

"Humph. Well, let me know if you hear from him. Did Bob say where Mr. Rue lived?"

"If he did, I didn't hear it, but I can call Stillman's radio and ask when they'll be back."

"Yeah, let's give it another half hour and then try."

"Sure thing. I heard from that guy again whose girlfriend disappeared."

"And did they make up and now everything is right with the world?"

Conway scratched his head. "Nope. According to the mother, who's disabled, Sally is still missing. The boyfriend is coming in soon to fill out a report."

Renz frowned. "That isn't good."

"No, sir, it isn't."

Renz returned to the office, spread the club applications out on the table, and looked them over again. He set aside the one for the member whose house he'd just been to.

"Now, what about the rest of you?" Renz tapped Drew Moore's application. He remembered Coltrane saying that he knew the guy. That left three others to check out. There was a Byron Price from Mechanicville, a Danny Simms from Houma, and a Robert Williams from Dulac. Renz rubbed his chin, stood, and returned to Conway's office.

"Excuse me, Pat, but did your deputies follow up with all those men who've had run-ins with the law?"

"Not sure, but I'll get you a list of the men they have spoken with."

"Okay, thanks. Just trying to narrow down the people that we haven't interviewed yet. There isn't time to repeat something that's already been done."

Back at the table, Renz paged through the notes they had taken over the last few days. There was still Teddy Cain, a local wife beater; mentally challenged Evan Millbrook, who wasn't home when they went calling; Derrick Alamane from Dulac, who liked to fight with cops; Destin Orly from McBride, who got paid for car repairs by jamming guns against people's temples; and Robby Williams, also from Dulac, who was a thief through and through and liked to beat anyone who called him out on it.

"Wait a minute. Robby Williams?"

Renz flipped through the applications again and pulled out the one for a Robert Williams.

What are the odds that he's the same person?

Renz ran his finger down the sheet. The gun club application showed Robert Williams as a Dulac resident.

"He has to be the same guy Leroy was talking about."

There weren't any photos included with the membership applications, so Renz logged on to the DMV database instead. If Robert Williams was willing to drive the half-hour distance from Dulac to Houma, he obviously had a vehicle and, Renz hoped, a valid driver's license. He typed in Robert Williams as the name and Dulac, Louisiana, as the city and state and then stared at the screen until the results popped up.

"Holy shit!" Renz leapt from his chair, nearly knocking it over, and ran to Conway's office. "Pat, we've got a problem. Bob Hebert isn't who he says he is. His real name is Robert Williams, he signed up Wednesday night as a new member at the hunting club, and he lives around Dulac. Leroy Duggar mentioned the name Robby Williams of Dulac as a possible person of interest, and now the son of a bitch has Jade."

"Damn it! Let's head out. I'll get Dispatch to see if anyone in Criminal Patrol is near that area since it's a half-hour drive for us. I need the address."

Renz handed Conway the application as they rushed down the hall to the dispatch counter. "Marie, get this address out to the criminal patrol unit. We need deputies on site ASAP. This Robert Williams character may be armed and dangerous, and he has Agent Monroe in his custody."

"On it, Boss."

Conway led the way to an available squad car. "I'll try Stillman's radio as we drive."

Renz slammed his fist against the dash. "I should have never let her go with him. I've had a weird feeling about that guy since day one."

"But Stillman went along. He and Jade are seasoned law enforcement officials and armed."

"Doesn't matter if you're blindsided."

The radio squawked, and Conway picked up. It was Marie getting back to him.

"Boss, the nearest unit said they're twenty minutes away."

"Shit! Okay, dispatch at least two deputies there and tell them to go in silent. We're on our way. Try Stillman's radio and get back to me. Keep trying every few minutes." Conway jerked his head toward Renz. "Do you think Williams is the killer?"

"That's one hundred percent what I think. We've got to get a warning out to Jade and Stillman."

Conway shook his head. "And they've already been there for more than an hour."

"Yeah, and that worries me even more."

They'd just reached the outskirts of Houma when the radio squawked again. It was Marie, and she said she couldn't get a response from Stillman.

Conway barked back into the radio. "Let me know the second those other units arrive."

Renz clenched his fists as Conway sped south down Grand Caillou Road en route to Dulac. He leaned over and gave the speedometer a glance. "Can't you go any faster?"

"Not if we actually want to arrive in one piece. There are too many small towns and businesses sprinkled along this road with cars pulling in and out. I'm going eighty miles an hour the way it is."

Seconds later, Marie radioed back. "Boss, the units just arrived and found Stillman's squad car parked in the middle of the driveway. He's dead, sir, with his throat slashed wide open."

Renz yelled out and pounded the dash again. "Shit! Tell those deputies to shoot Robert Williams on sight, no questions asked. My partner's life is in his hands."

Chapter 51

My head pounded from the beating Bob had given me. My vision seemed blurred—I chalked it up to a concussion. I looked around and did my best to get a clear focus but couldn't see him anywhere. What I could see and smell was wood burning and a roaring fire coming from the pit several hundred feet away.

Where did you go, Bob?

I assumed he went into one of the sheds, likely to get his tools of the trade—killing, carving, and cutting knives. I couldn't believe that I'd fallen for his ploy of helping the FBI while all along, he was reeling me in hook, line, and sinker. Now it was my turn to die, and nobody knew where I was.

That means if I don't save myself, I'll be in hot water—literally—before the day is over.

A branch snapped at my back, but I couldn't see around the tree. I was sure a gator had seen an opportunity and would have me for a meal before Bob got the chance.

"Psst."

I jerked my head to the side. What kind of sick game

was he playing? Was Bob coming up from behind to slit my throat like he'd done to Stillman?

"Who's there?"

"My name is Sally. Troy kidnapped me and beat me into unconsciousness. I was tied to this tree all night, but I escaped just before dawn. I've been hiding in the swamp, and when he left earlier, I started working my way back to the house. I prayed there would be a phone inside. I was getting close, but then he returned. I saw what he was doing to you and hid again. Where do you think he went?"

"I don't know where anyone is, but I need you to untie me and fast. I'm an FBI agent, and we have to get the hell out of here. Please, hurry!" Just then, a gunshot rang out. "Oh my God! Please, get these ropes off of me!"

"I'm scared!"

"I am, too, Sally, but damn it, you need to get these ropes off of me now. I can protect you but only if we're both free!"

Sally worked frantically on the ropes while I kept my eyes peeled for Bob to return. Seconds later, I heard another gunshot then silence.

"Hurry!"

"Okay, your hands are free. Let's get your legs."

My head throbbed as I knelt over to untie the ropes from my ankles. That was my first look at Sally, and by her appearance, Bob had worked her over badly. She was lucky to be alive.

Free from my restraints, I saw the hammer still lying in the dirt. I picked it up and led the way.

"Come on, Sally. Run like your life depends on it because it does. He has my gun and probably plenty more. We've got nothing but our wits. Don't get too close to the water, though. As far as I know, gators don't wander inland too far, but there's still snakes and wild hogs. Watch every step you take, but you have to keep right at my side, and we have to run until our lungs ache."

As I thought about the property layout and the location of the driveway, I knew the road had to be on our left. We would run straight for a while then veer in that direction. I didn't want to be anywhere close to Bob's driveway or give him the opportunity to see us running through the woods from the upper floor of his house. My mind raced as we ran. I remembered Bob bragging about being a great hunter and tracker and wondered how true that was. He'd left me alone at the tree for quite a while as he built that fire, but then he'd disappeared, and within minutes, the gunshot rang out and, seconds after, another. He either saw or heard something that raised his suspicions. I hoped to God law enforcement had arrived, but at the same time, I hoped they hadn't. If those shots I'd heard were aimed at unsuspecting targets, then it, or they, were probably dead, just like Stillman.

"Okay, let's stop for a second and catch our breath." I looked down and saw Sally's bloody foot. "What the hell happened to your shoe?"

"I lost it this morning in the mud and couldn't find it again. It was still dark outside."

"Here," I whispered. I took off my shoe and gave it to

her. "You need it more than I do right now." I put my finger to my mouth then cocked my ear. I didn't hear anything yet—no twigs snapping or anyone running through the woods. That told me there was a chance that Bob hadn't noticed I was gone yet. "Okay, come on. We still have to get farther away before we cut over to the road."

"What if he's driving back and forth and sees us?"

"We'll stay in the woods but close enough to be parallel to the road. I know Bob's truck, and if I see it, we'll duck down."

"He said his name was Troy."

"I know, honey, but he's probably given a fake name to everyone he's abducted. Come on. We have to keep moving."

We continued on, and I heard Bob yell out. He'd discovered that I was gone. My heart pounded, and I knew he would be even more dangerous if he caught up to us. No matter what, I couldn't let him know that Sally was still alive.

"Jade, oh, Jade. Where the hell are you? You know as soon as I locate your tracks, I'll find you. I know these swamps much better than you do, and I know what predators lurk here."

His words gave me goose bumps. He had given me a warning earlier, which I'd brushed off as trivia. Man was the most dangerous predator, and he was proving it with every step he took into the swamp.

"You aren't leaving here alive, and the deputies who just showed up aren't either. They've already met the same fate Stillman did, and don't forget, I have your gun as well as a rifle. If I see you in the woods and put a bead on you, you're as good as dead."

We crouched down and didn't move a muscle. I could tell by Bob's voice that he was still a ways off, but if we began to run frantically through the woods, the noise would give away our location.

I whispered to Sally, who was quickly becoming unglued, to take a deep breath and stay calm. Then I heard Renz holler my name. A rush of relief mixed with fear swept over me. The cavalry had arrived, but they had no idea what they were heading into.

Chapter 52

Renz saw the doors open and ran to the squad car. Nobody was there. He and Conway inched forward and found both deputies lying on the ground next to Stillman's car. They'd been shot dead, and by the looks of it, they hadn't seen it coming. Neither had drawn their guns.

"Good God! I have three dead deputies here. What kind of maniac are we dealing with?"

"The worst kind, Pat." Renz knelt and put two fingers against the neck of the deputy lying on his side of the squad car. He shook his head. "He's definitely gone." Renz looked around. "Robert Williams is cunning, clever, and cautious. These deputies didn't know they were being watched, and that tells me Robert is using a rifle. We have to stay low and remain in the tree cover."

"But he already knows we're here. You yelled out to Jade."

"That's right, but between her, you, and me, we can outsmart him."

"What makes you think Jade is still alive?"

Renz watched his surroundings as they advanced. "Stay

under the trees, Pat. Don't walk on the driveway. If Jade was dead, Robert would have taken off after shooting the deputies. He'd know that we were onto him, and there wouldn't be a reason for him to stick around. Jade is out here somewhere and now it's a matter of finding her."

They weaved through the woods with their guns drawn. With the small amount of daylight glowing between the trees, Renz saw the buildings.

"We're almost to the clearing. I can see the outbuildings and house from here. It's going to be tricky getting from the woods to the buildings without being shot at, but we have to check those sheds and the house before we go any farther."

"We need backup."

Renz shrugged. "Go ahead and call, but we don't have a half hour to wait. We need to find Jade now." The larger building appeared to be a garage, and it was the closest to the tree line, a hundred feet away, but a hundred feet without cover. They would have to make a run for it. "Are you ready?"

They scanned the surroundings and every window in sight. They didn't see any movement. Conway gave Renz a nod.

"Okay, on three. Three, two, one, go!"

They bolted for the garage then hugged the wall when they reached it. Renz crouched at the window and slowly stood until he could see in. A tarp-covered truck sat inside. He turned the knob, and the door squeaked open. They entered cautiously and cleared the space. Renz yanked the tarp off the truck and saw Billy's red Dodge Ram underneath.

"Shit. So that son of a bitch played along as Lorna Bennett cried for her husband's safe return. That man is beyond evil."

Renz looked out the window. The house was the next building, directly across from the garage, and a smaller shed, likely for tools and yard equipment, sat on the edge of the woods on the far side of the driveway.

"We aren't going into the house, are we?" Conway asked.

Renz shook his head. "We better not since that could be a death sentence. There's only one way in and one way out, and we'd be completely exposed. He could pick us off like birds on a wire."

"So then what?"

"Then we need to find a way to draw him out. Let's get to the house, peer around the back where the stairs are, and see what's there. If we don't spot Jade anywhere, I'll keep yelling out to her. Either Robert will get sidetracked and come after us, he'll yell back, which would give us an indication of where he's at, or he'll shoot in our direction, so we have to be protected by cover. If he's here, which I think he is, he's either in the house or in the swamp—and neither are good for us."

They rushed to the back of the house. Renz peeked around the corner while Conway covered his back.

"I don't see anyone anywhere. The only thing I do see is a roaring fire with a big metal pot over it. He's got to be out there somewhere since that fire has recently been tended."

"There isn't any way to get to the tree cover on the other side without running through the clearing," Conway said as he took a look. "If he's in the house, he'll pick us off in seconds, but we can't start shooting at the house to force him out if Jade is inside too."

"Yeah, I know. All I can do is yell her name and wait for an answer—"

Conway raised his hand. "Yell his name instead. Jade isn't going to give up her location if by some miracle she was able to get away from him."

"You're right, and if he's the narcissist I think he is, he won't be able to resist my taunts. We'll be able to track down his location by his voice." Renz cupped his hands around his mouth and yelled Robert's name. "Robert Williams! We know who you are and what you've done. There's no way out. You can only stay in the swamp for so long before the animals take you out. Instead of the hunter, you'll be the hunted. Your days of killing people are over. Now throw down your weapons and come out. We will shoot to kill and that's a promise." They waited for the response they needed. It was the only way to zero in on his location. It seemed like forever, but he finally yelled back.

"Nope, not doing it, Agent DeLeon. What do I have to lose by staying out in the swamps? You'll never come in here to find me. You don't have the stones."

"Well, apparently, Jade does. You wouldn't be out there unless you were looking for her. Guess she got away from you, right?"

"I like to hunt, and Agent Monroe is my prey. She's

going to be my trophy kill, and then you're next. The best part is you won't even see it coming, just like those deputies didn't. Doubt if your handguns are any competition for my rifle."

Renz pointed at the woods. They would have to get ahead of Robert then work their way back. The bayou was on one side and filled with alligators. The road was on the other side, and hopefully, help was on the way. Somewhere in between were Jade and the monster tracking her.

"Let's take the road, Conway. We can get ahead of him and then backtrack through the woods. If we try to go straight in, he'll mow us down in a matter of seconds."

"Shouldn't we check the house first?"

"No, going up those stairs is still too dangerous. He can easily pick us off with that rifle, especially if it has a scope on it. He wouldn't be out in that swamp unless Jade was too. He's already admitted that." Renz jerked his head toward the driveway. "Let's take the squad car up the road a half mile or so, see what the ETA is for our backup, and then head into the woods on foot."

Chapter 53

We heard the exchange between Renz and Bob. I now knew that his real name was Robert Williams, and it was apparent that Renz had figured out everything he needed to know about the man. From what Robert had said, he wasn't going to stop coming after me. If Sally and I went to the road and he saw us through the trees, he would have an easy shot with that rifle. We had to stay in the dense cover—it was our only way to survive. I doubted that he would expect us to head toward the water. It was too dangerous with alligators along the banks, just waiting for an unsuspecting animal to come down to drink. *What I'd give for a drink of water.* I was sure Sally was even thirstier, but we would hold out. We didn't have a choice.

"We need to go deeper into the swamp, Sally."

"Why? I thought we were going to head toward the road."

"He has that rifle, and it's too dangerous in open areas. We need to stay as invisible as possible. My partner will find us sooner or later, and I'm sure backup is already on the way."

That time, we moved slowly. I didn't want to give away our location, and I knew Robert was closing in. If only I had my phone so I could tell Renz where we were, but we didn't have that luxury. I was going on my wits, and I had to do whatever I could to outsmart Robert Williams.

The ground became squishier, and keeping our shoes on was nearly impossible. The mud nearly sucked off the only shoe I was wearing, and then I understood how easy it was for Sally to lose hers that morning. The mosquitos and bugs were relentless, and the bites were constant. I did my best to keep the slapping at a minimum so Robert wouldn't hear it. We were becoming tangled in vines, and the closer we got to the water, the more fearful I became. Maybe that direction was the wrong choice. From where we were, I could see the bayou and the large cypress trees jutting out of the water. Shivers ran up my spine at the loud commotion and the screech of a bird likely getting eaten by a gator, but I had to stay levelheaded to keep us alive.

"We're going to stay right here and hunker down until help arrives. This fallen log will hide us." I looked Sally straight in the eyes. "No matter what, we can't scream if we see something that terrifies us like an enormous spider." I held up the hammer. "Remember, we have this if we need to use it."

It wasn't long before I heard movement, and it was getting closer. I felt Sally tense up as she sat against me. I put my finger to my mouth. "Shh." I couldn't say anything else for fear that he'd hear me. I was sure I'd made the wrong decision. We should have gone to the road. Barely moving,

I peeked around the log and saw him. He was to our right and a hundred feet away. I was sure if he passed us and looked back, he would see us. The only thing I could think of was to camouflage ourselves the best we could. I quietly picked up a glob of mud and spread it over Sally's face and hair. I gave her a nod to continue smearing it on her clothes while I did the same. I knew nothing about survival skills in the swamp, but I assumed the mud might hide our scent too. I indicated for her to lie flat, even as disgusting as that was, and I smeared mud over the back of her clothes. I gave her the hammer then heard a crackling sound just beyond the log. I was afraid to move, but I had to. I looked up and saw the rifle barrel a foot from my head.

"Get up, bitch. I knew I'd find you. It was just a matter of who has the better skills, and smearing mud over yourself apparently didn't do it. I could still smell the perfume you probably doused yourself in this morning."

He waved the rifle at me. "I told you to stand up!"

I did as told and stepped over the log so he wouldn't see Sally.

"Where the hell do you think you're going?"

"I figured you were taking me back to the house."

"You figured wrong. All the stress and running through the woods? Your meat is garbage now. You're gator food, not good for anything else."

My eyes darted left and right as I searched the woods for Renz. I didn't see anything other than Robert and his rifle.

He chuckled. "This was a great hunt, Jade. You might be wasted meat, but you'll still be a trophy in my mind."

He waved the barrel at me. "Head for the water."

"What! You can't be serious." I looked over my shoulder and saw the bayou thirty feet at my back.

"I'm dead serious, or should I say you'll just be dead." He grinned. "This has been fun, and as soon as you're out of the way, I'll tend to the others." He jerked his head. "Now keep going. I want you at the edge of the water so you can see the gators for yourself. They'll be licking their chops at the sight of you."

I backed up slowly, hoping to hell that Renz would see Robert and fire a shot, but nothing happened.

"Go on. You're almost there."

I looked back again—only ten feet from the water's edge.

"Can you see their eyeballs sticking out of the water? They're waiting for you, Jade, so it's your choice. Shall I shoot you first or make you wade out to them so they can devour you while you're still alive? That would be quite the show and just picturing it is almost erotic."

"You're a sick son of a bitch." I kept backing up as he nudged me with the barrel of the rifle. My eye caught movement behind Robert—it was Sally.

"That's truer than you know. My mother was a bitch and a crazy one at that." Robert spun when a twig snapped at his back.

With the hammer lifted high, Sally brought it down on his head with such force that I heard his skull crack. She screamed her rage and pushed him with all her might. Robert dropped the rifle, stumbled backward, and fell into the bayou. A frenzy of opportunistic alligators descended on him, and as they thrashed and ripped his body apart, the water turned blood red.

I squeezed Sally with all my might. "You just saved my life, and I'll never forget that." I picked up the rifle, glanced back briefly at the red-tinted water, then looked away. "Come on, honey. Let's get the hell out of here." As we moved to safer ground, I lifted the rifle and fired off a few rounds above the water then yelled out Renz's name. Relief washed over me when I heard his reply.

"Stay put, Jade. We'll come to you."

"I have Sally too. We're both okay, but get us the hell out of this swamp."

It took another ten minutes before I saw Renz, Conway, and two deputies I didn't recognize heading our way. I heard sirens approaching in the distance. We were safe and would be okay, but my heart ached for the deputies who had been shot. I let out a long groan when Renz and the others reached us.

"You're a sight for sore eyes, DeLeon."

Renz shook his head. "And you're just a sight. I can't tell if either if you are injured or not with that mud slathered all over your bodies, but we have several ambulances on the way." Renz looked around. "What happened to Robert Williams?"

I let out a relieved sigh. "Poetic justice."

Chapter 54

It was Sunday, the day we would have been leaving, anyway. Luckily, the killings were over, the case was solved, and Robert Williams was no longer a threat to society or to Terrebonne Parish. Our flight wasn't until later that day, and we had a lot to wrap up before we left. Detectives and deputies from the Criminal Patrol Unit searched the property and found all the IDs from Robert's victims in an envelope in the glove box of his truck. I couldn't believe I'd sat in that truck and only inches from proof of his guilt and didn't know it. Renz told me not to be so hard on myself since without me giving Bob a chance to help us, we might never have learned that he was the killer. No matter what, it was over, and he'd gotten what he deserved.

The deputies said there was evidence in the woods of where Billy and Mark were likely killed by wild pigs. According to their account, the men might have been tied to trees in the pigs' nesting area. The thought sickened me, and I couldn't imagine what Lorna would have to go through in the coming weeks and months. She would never have closure.

"What's going to happen to the pets?" I asked Conway as we sat in our makeshift office.

"One of the deputies took the dog home, and the cats went to a local shelter." He gave me a long stare. "You sure you're okay? Your face is really black and blue."

I waved off his comment. "I'm more concerned about Sally, but the doctor said she'd be okay. I've been black and blue plenty of times, so I'll be fine. I intend to visit Sally before we leave town, though."

"She's a brave young lady," Conway said.

My eyes began to pool. "Damn straight she is. Sally saved my life. It would have likely been me who was eaten by those gators instead of Robert."

Conway huffed. "That sick bastard got everything he deserved and more. The crime lab took all the meat out of his coolers. They're pretty sure it's of the human variety, but more testing is needed to be certain. Cash was found in the house, and remnants of melted credit cards, buttons, zippers, and purses were discovered in the ash from the firepit."

"So he killed people for food and money. I imagine what he said about the job he had was also false."

With a puff of air, Conway continued, "Robert Williams hasn't been gainfully employed for years. The only income he had was by leasing out his land to the state for hunters to use."

"How about donating his land to the hunting club, then?"

Conway rubbed his chin. "That could be a possibility.

It'll take some time to sort through everything and contact all the families. They may want a settlement for the death of their loved one, and selling off the property could help with that."

Renz nodded. "I'm just glad this case is closed since I don't like the idea of going home without a resolution."

I agreed wholeheartedly. "That makes two of us. We'll have to sign off on the case after you guys wrap up everything. You'll overnight the paperwork to us?"

"Absolutely, but I'll contact you every few days to let you know of our progress and what will be done with his land."

"Sounds like a plan. We should go pack and check out of the hotel." Renz looked at me. "And then you want to spend some time with Sally before we go, right?"

"Definitely. She invited us to her house to meet her mama and boyfriend. She said they'd made up, and he'd be there too."

Renz shook Conway's hand, then I took my turn as we said our goodbyes. "Pat, we're so sorry about your deputies. You and their families have our deepest condolences."

"Thanks, Jade, and thanks to both of you for getting that maniac out of our lives. Our hearts will heal, but it'll take some time."

We returned to the hotel to pack. I told Renz I would meet him in the lobby in twenty minutes. We planned to check out, have lunch, and visit Sally before leaving for the airport. Louisiana had probably seen the last of us for some time, but I had memories that would endure forever. The people were good folks all around, and anyone who thought otherwise just misunderstood them, like we initially did. I laughed at the memory of Leroy Duggar as I packed. That man scared the bejesus out of me until we made peace around his firepit. Those people just wanted to live their lives by their own rules, not ours. I respected that.

In the bathroom, I started putting my toiletries in my cosmetic bag. I picked up the perfume bottle and stared at it, then I shook my head and dropped it into the garbage can. Little by little, I'd learned valuable lessons over the years.

I zipped my backpack and go bag, looked around the room, then walked out. I met Renz downstairs, and he said he'd already checked us out. I placed my key cards on the counter, and we left.

"Where to for lunch?"

"The scooter store."

Renz raised his brows. "Excuse me?"

I grinned. "Well, there *is* a phone store and a diner in that same strip mall. The food at the diner is supposed to be good. I've already checked it out online."

"Back to the scooter comment. What am I missing here?"

I let out a long breath. "After talking more to Sally, I learned that her mom is disabled from diabetes. She can't walk worth a shit, and her wheelchair is old and has seen better days."

"Yeah, Conway said the boyfriend had mentioned that the mom was disabled." Renz grinned. "So what's the plan?"

"I'm buying the mom a scooter so she can get out of the house and enjoy life with Sally."

"It sounds like a *but* is coming."

"Not a *but*. More like an *and*."

"Okay, *and* what?"

"And I opened an online bank account in Sally's name. I'm going to put five hundred bucks a month in it until she's twenty-five. It's the least I can do, and it'll give her a head start in life. They don't have a lot, Renz."

He held up his hands. "There's no way I'd try to talk you out of that. You've got a good heart, Jade."

"My dad taught us well."

"You know, we've got a three-hour flight back to Milwaukee. I'd like to hear more about your family."

I smiled. "You sure? I've got a lot to share."

He nodded. "I'm sure."

Renz turned in to the strip mall's parking lot. "What do you want to do first?"

"Let's get the scooter and phone, and then we'll eat after that. Can you give me just a minute, though? I'd like to call Amber if I can use your phone."

"You bet." He handed it to me and climbed out of the Explorer.

I watched as Renz stepped up to the sidewalk and sat on the bench outside the scooter store. I dialed Amber's number, and she picked up right away.

"Hello?"

"Hey, Sis."

"Hey. Whose phone are you using?"

I sighed. "It's Renz's. Mine got eaten by an alligator."

"You aren't serious, are you?"

"I'm pretty sure I am. Do you know what the most dangerous predator is, Amber?"

"Of course I do. It's man."

"Good, and don't ever forget that."

"I hope you're heading home. You sound exhausted."

"We are, and I am. We'll be leaving in a few hours. I have so much to tell you and Kate."

"So the case is closed?"

"Yes. We got the bad guy, and that's what counts. Remember what I requested for supper a few days ago?"

"Yep. Meat loaf, mashed potatoes, and corn on the cob. So you'll be home for supper?"

"I sure will, and I can't wait. I love you, Sis."

"And I love you too. Now hang up so I can go to the grocery store."

I grinned, hung up, and met Renz at the door of the scooter store. I didn't know what color scooter to buy, but when I thought about Sally's mud-stained pink shorts, my mind was made up. I loved pink, Sally loved pink, and I was sure her mom would love pink too.

THE END

Thank you!

Thanks for reading *Blood in the Bayou*, the first book in the new FBI Agent Jade Monroe Live or Die Series. I hope you enjoyed it!

Find all my books leading up to this series at http://cmsutter.com

Stay abreast of my new releases by signing up for my VIP email list at: http://cmsutter.com/newsletter/

You'll be one of the first to get a glimpse of the cover reveals and release dates, and you'll have a chance at exciting raffles offered with each new release.

Posting a review will help other readers find my books. I appreciate every review, whether positive or negative, and if you have a second to spare, a review is truly appreciated.

Find me on Facebook at
https://www.facebook.com/cmsutterauthor/

Printed in Dunstable, United Kingdom